GIVE ME MURDER

Give Me Murder

A Patrick Dawlish Mystery

**John Creasey *writing as*
Gordon Ashe**

ISBN: 978-1-5040-9880-9

This edition published in 2025 by Open Road Integrated Media, Inc.
180 Maiden Lane
New York, NY 10038
www.openroadmedia.com

GIVE ME MURDER

CHAPTER ONE

THE MYSTERIOUS MR. GALLOWAY

A Rolls-Royce drew up outside the Marine Hotel at Highsea. The manager appeared on the porch; and he was smiling.

The chauffeur helped a man out of the Rolls-Royce.

He was rather small and tubby. He was dressed in a light-grey tweed suit with tiny red and yellow spots, and wore a colourful tie. His fair hair was fluffy and stirred by the sea breeze. His brown shoes shone in the sun.

The manager actually walked down the steps to greet him.

"Good afternoon, Mr. Galloway! I do hope you have had a comfortable journey."

"Eh?" ejaculated Galloway. "Oh, yes, thank you." He smiled. "Kind of you to inquire," he declared.

"I am very glad that I have been able to give you a first-floor suite, Mr. Galloway."

"Kind," murmured Galloway; "most kind."

The manager asked him whether he would like to sign the register, he took up a pen which was thrust towards him by one of the receptionists, who said in a small voice:

"Good afternoon, Mr. Galloway."

"Oh, good afternoon," said Galloway. He poised the pen and looked at the girl. She was young and comely. He smiled again.

By that time his chauffeur and the porters were in the hall with his luggage. There was one cabin trunk, three large pigskin travelling cases and several small cases.

"Would you like tea here, in one of the lounges, or in the quiet of your room?" asked the manager.

"I will have tea down here, in that chair, I think." He pointed to a chair which was facing the reception desk, and seemed to wink.

"You would like to wash first, I'm sure," said the manager.

"Oh, yes, please," said Mr. Galloway. "Yes, thank you."

In the manager's wake, he toddled off towards the lift.

Except for the staff, the only witnesses to the incidents in the hall were a man and a woman sitting by an open window. The man was remarkable for his size; even when sitting down he gave the impression of being a giant. The sun shone on his crisp, fair hair, into his cornflower-blue eyes, on to his large face. Had it not been for his broad, broken nose he would have been a good-looking man. As it was, there was something attractive about his appearance. Already, although he had been at the Marine only for three days, he was a first favourite with the staff.

His name was Dawlish, and although he was entitled to call himself 'Major', he preferred to be known as Mr. Patrick Dawlish.

Equally popular with the staff was Mrs. Dawlish. She sat by his side, with one leg resting on a footstool. The leg was shapely and silk-clad. She wore a soft green linen dress, trimmed with lemon-coloured silk. She was not particularly good-looking, but her face was friendly and pleasant, and her very large grey-green eyes were beautiful. Her hair was wavy and a little untidy; she looked fresh and delightful as the breeze stirred the curls at the nape of her neck.

"Well," murmured Dawlish, leaning towards her.

"Most unexpected," said his wife.

"Nothing like the mysterious Mr. Galloway we had been led to expect."

"No," admitted Felicity Dawlish. "In fact, if we hadn't known what we do about him I would have called him a dear."

"It's going to be difficult to see him in the rôle of double-dyed villain," said Dawlish.

"Does that mean you're weakening?" demanded Felicity.

"Certainly not," said Dawlish. "No man can rob me of eleven thousand pounds and get away with it."

"When you say 'rob', darling," chided Felicity, "wouldn't it be better if you made sure that no one could hear you?"

"Only you are within earshot."

"The window's open," his wife reminded him.

"So it is," said Dawlish, glancing round with an air of surprise, "but I doubt whether my whisper travelled outside."

"Your whisper is another man's shout," Felicity told him.

Normally, he was a man who liked to say what he thought. That did not mean, however, that he was inconsiderate. On the subject of financial geniuses like Mr. Galloway, nevertheless, he was remarkably outspoken. He had not talked idly when he said that Mr. Galloway had 'robbed' him of eleven thousand pounds. Admittedly it had been legal robbery. Dawlish even admitted that; he should not have invested the money in a company about which he knew so little.

The worst feature of that financial loss was that it represented a large proportion of his fortune. It had not ruined him, but it was serious.

Felicity was following that train of thought.

"Don't you think we're likely to waste our time?" she asked. "We might only throw good money after bad. If Galloway is as rich as he's supposed to be, he'll be much too strong for us."

"Does money make strength?" demanded Dawlish.

"Yes, in such cases as this," answered Felicity.

"I thought better of you," reproached Dawlish. "You were as angry as I when it happened. True, you were more high-souled. 'Think less of our own loss,' you said, 'than that of the thousands of other people, many of whom have lost their all.' Oh, indisputably, you were most indignant," continued Dawlish, with obvious enjoyment at the sight of his wife's expression. "You were anxious for me to take on the rôle of Robin Hood; protector of the poor. In fact, if I remember rightly, you were so angry that you insisted I must do something about it, there and then."

"Well, didn't you?"

"Only under your pressure," answered Dawlish. "I made inquiries among the police, and found that nothing was known about our Mr. Galloway, except his indecent wealth. I say indecent, but the police didn't. There was, in fact, no chance at all of getting legal revenge. Still you persisted. 'After all you've done,' your pet phrase seemed to be—'after all you've done, you're going to sit back and take this. Shame on you!'"

"You wouldn't be exaggerating at all, would you?" asked Felicity.

"Not a scrap," declared Dawlish. "Here we are at the Marine, staying at enormous expense which we can ill afford, in the hope of learning more, if we can, about Galloway—perhaps even approaching him, telling him the sad story of those unfortunates who have lost their all and of us few fools who lost a great deal, to see whether the milk of human kindness has or has not dried up in his breast. He looks as if he's oozing with it. Hallo, here he comes—no, it's a waiter. Special tea for Mr. Galloway, I imagine."

A table was pulled to the side of the chair which Galloway had indicated, and a waiter put cups and saucers, bread and butter, pastries and cakes on it, then stood back to examine the result. He moved a spoon here, a small knife there, stood back again, and appeared to give it his approbation. Off he walked.

From where Dawlish and Felicity were sitting they could see only part of the table. Their settee was in a corner, for they had not wanted Mr. Galloway to see them when he first entered. Dawlish preferred to be able to size up the other side first. As a result, the performance of the waiter had been irritating, because they had seen him part of the time, but only his hands at other times.

The hall, during those few moments, was empty so far as the Dawlishes could see.

Then Dawlish heard a movement. He was still looking towards Galloway's table. He saw a hand and a coat-sleeve hover for a moment above the table. It seemed to him something dropped from the hand, which was immediately withdrawn.

Dawlish swung to his feet, made a warning sign to Felicity, and hurried across the hall. As he did so the doors opened and a stream of people came in. One moment the hall had been practically empty, the next it was filled with a gay, chattering crowd.

The man whose hand had hovered over Galloway's table had been wearing a dark coat, and three of the men now in the hall wore dark coats.

Dawlish went back to Felicity.

"What on earth is the matter with you?" she demanded.

"Didn't you see it?"

"See what?"

"The hand."

"What hand?"

"A man dropped something into Galloway's sugar bowl or the milk jug. I don't know which."

She looked up at him sharply. There was a change in him, one which she had seen only too often. His expression was hard, he was very much on the alert.

"Who was it?" she asked, in a low-pitched voice.

"I couldn't see. The crowd beat me," Dawlish told her. "Interesting development, isn't it, sweet? Someone wants Galloway to take something that isn't good for him. I've no love for Mr. Galloway, but I don't think anyone should tamper with his tea. The question is, how best to deal with the situation?"

"Please don't make a scene," pleaded Felicity, "I—"

Then she broke off, for Galloway, beaming broadly, stepped out of the lift and walked to his table.

CHAPTER TWO

SPILT MILK

This time Galloway's entrance was an anticlimax. The new-comers did not know who he was. Galloway sat down. Dawlish squeezed Felicity's arm, and said:

"I'll be good."

He asked the porter for some cigarettes, put them in his pocket, and turned round. A waiter was about to pour out Galloway's tea. Dawlish stumbled. The waiter saw him falling, and backed away. Dawlish strove to recover his balance and swept his arms out. He knocked both milk and sugar off the table.

Galloway looked at him apprehensively. Dawlish towered over him. The waiter rushed forward, seeing the pool of milk disappearing into the carpet and the knobs of sugar dotted all about.

"I am *really* sorry," said Dawlish.

"My dear sir, don't worry about it," said Galloway. "I am not hurt."

"I stumbled," said Dawlish.

"So I observed," declared Galloway.

"I think it must have been the edge of the carpet," said Dawlish, and searched the floor. The carpet had no edge just there. He watched the waiter picking up the sugar. He intended to get possession of that sugar, for he badly wanted to know what was in it.

"I will bring some fresh milk and sugar, sir," said the waiter.

"I am in no hurry," said Galloway, benignly.

"Very kind of you," murmured Dawlish. "My wife will be most angry with me. Put in a word for me, if you get the chance, Dawlish is the name." Then he went off quickly in the wake of the waiter.

Galloway looked about him, and caught Felicity's eyes. His own eyes lit up, as they always did when he saw an attractive woman. He beckoned another waiter.

"Which is Mrs. Dawlish?" he asked.

"The lady on the settee, sir."

Galloway got up and walked over to Felicity, who was taken completely by surprise.

Dawlish, meanwhile, followed the waiter.

He knew a little of the lay-out of the Marine Hotel. It was his habit to get to know all that he could about the exits and entrances of an hotel, a habit which had been forced upon him. He found himself in a narrow passage where several doors were standing ajar. He caught a glimpse of the tails of the waiter's coat disappearing into one of the rooms. He followed. It was a large pantry, where two women were pouring milk into tiny jugs and putting sugar into basins.

"Great clumsy lout," grumbled the waiter. "Better give me a fresh lot," he said; "put this with the other."

"I am so sorry about it," murmured Dawlish.

The waiter and the two women jumped and swung round. Dawlish beamed at them. The waiter coloured, and was speechless.

"And you are quite right, waiter, I was clumsy."

The waiter went turkey red.

"However, no great harm is done," continued Dawlish. "I'll have a word with the manager if you like." He leaned against the counter, and his coat covered the sugar which had come from Galloway's table.

He picked the little bowl up and hid it in his great hand. Dawlish beamed again, and walked out.

His own room was on the fifth floor, and soon Dawlish was examining the sugar in front of his window.

There seemed nothing wrong with it.

As he peered more closely, however, Dawlish saw a little white powder on it. There was a little of the powder at the bottom of the bowl, too.

"It'll have to be examined properly," he murmured aloud.

He wrapped the bowl in a handkerchief, put it in an attaché case, and went downstairs. He did not need to cross the main hall to get out. As he passed the hall window, however, he heard Felicity talking, and her voice was followed immediately by the honeyed tones of Mr. Galloway. Dawlish grinned as he turned out of the gateway towards the shopping centre, which was only a minute's walk away.

He turned into the first chemist's shop, where a well-dressed girl in a pink smock greeted him.

"I would like a word with the chief dispenser, please," said Dawlish.

"I won't keep you a moment, sir."

Soon, at the far end of the shop, behind the dispensary, Dawlish and a short, harassed-looking man engaged in earnest conversation. Dawlish explained that he had reason to believe that something had been poured over the sugar. Naturally, he wanted to be sure, and it occurred to him that the chemist would analyse the sugar for him.

"Well, yes, I could," admitted the chemist. "But what do you think is on it?"

"It might be a harmless powder, in which case it was a practical joke and I needn't worry about it. On the other hand, it *might* prove to be dangerous drug. I think I ought to know, don't you?"

"The *police* ought to know, you mean."

"Oh, undoubtedly, if it is a poison," said Dawlish, "but I don't want to worry them if it's harmless."

"I see what you mean," said the dispenser. "It will take me an hour. If it is a drug, I'll have to tell the police."

Dawlish gave the man his card. "Tell the police I brought it in, and that I'm staying at the Marine. Ask them to telephone me first and not call in person."

He left the shop and strolled back to the hotel.

He went in by the main entrance—and there, at Mr. Galloway's table, sat Felicity. Mr. Galloway was talking quickly and behaving gallantly.

Galloway jumped up, gaily.

"Waiter! Another chair."

The waiter brought the chair and laid another place.

They took a long time over tea.

The page-boy approached, calling a name. As he drew nearer, Dawlish heard his own being called.

"Telephone call for Mr. Dawlish," said the boy.

Dawlish went to the telephone-box and picked up the receiver. An agitated voice sounded in his ear.

"I *must* speak to Mr. Dawlish, *at once.*"

"Dawlish speaking."

"This is Morrison—the dispenser from the chemist's."

"Yes?"

"It was *strychnine.*"

"Was it, by George!"

"You can't take it as calmly as that!" cried Morrison. "It is a deadly poison; there was enough to kill a dozen men! I must tell the police at once!"

"Yes, of course you must," said Dawlish. "You will ask them to telephone me, won't you?"

"I—oh! Oh, yes." The man seemed startled, for no reason at all. "I shall speak to the Superintendent personally."

It was warm in the booth, but Dawlish did not think that accounted for the sweat on his forehead, the warmth he felt. There was something sinister about the quickness of the attempt to murder Galloway. The question was whether to tell Galloway about it before he saw the police.

It dawned upon him then, belatedly, that he had been presented with a remarkable opportunity for worming himself into Galloway's good graces.

He looked across the hall.

Galloway was getting up, still talking earnestly to Felicity. He even rested a hand on Felicity's arm. Felicity smiled, without much enthusiasm. Galloway patted her hand, and then went towards the stairs.

Dawlish drew up as he disappeared.

"Doing well, honey?" he asked, facetiously.

"Pat, you're impossible!"

"*I'm* impossible!" protested Dawlish. "*You've* made all the running. And he patted your hand, too. Let me touch the spot where the finger of a millionaire lingered."

"Oh, don't be an ass!"

"Now I've some news for you. There was something sprinkled over his sugar. Nasty stuff. If he'd swallowed any of it, the Marine would be mourning its most honoured guest."

Felicity paled.

"It's a fact," murmured Dawlish. "I've a chemist's word for it.

He is now telephoning the police. I wonder what the police are like in Highsea."

"I can hardly believe it," said Felicity.

"It's true," Dawlish repeated. "Someone else came here to take revenge on Galloway. With our motive, we might have been suspect. Isn't it lucky I saw the hand and the sleeve?"

"What are you going to do?"

"First of all I'm going to interview our Mr. Galloway, and then I've no doubt the police will want a word with me, and after that—who knows?"

"If I'd *dreamed* anything like this would happen, I would not have come," declared Felicity, hotly. "Pat, *must* you become mixed up in a thing like this?"

"It looks as if I *am* mixed up in it," Dawlish observed, "but I might get squeezed out."

"Yes," she said, "let's hope you will be!"

"And if a call comes through for me, answer it and say I'll be free in half an hour, will you?" asked Dawlish, and went towards the stairs.

A maid came out of a first-floor room.

"Where can I find Mr. Galloway?" asked Dawlish.

"Oh, that's the *other* way, sir—in the west wing. He's in Suite 3."

The door was near the end of the passage. The window at the end overlooked Highsea Bay and the island which lay just offshore. He paused a moment to look at the silent scene, and then rang the bell. The door was opened promptly by a small, well-dressed man with a nondescript face.

"Yes?" he said, brusquely.

"Is Mr. Galloway in?" asked Dawlish, as abruptly.

"Who wants to see him?"

"I do. My name is Dawlish." The man annoyed him, but there

was no point in giving vent to his annoyance. "Tell him the matter is urgent, will you?"

The man appeared to be reluctant, but allowed Dawlish to enter the hall-lounge of the suite. It was excellently furnished, and had a great window overlooking the bay. The well-dressed man, whose clothes were dark, went into a room on the right. Before long he came out again and beckoned Dawlish.

From the door Dawlish saw Galloway sitting in an easy chair and smoking. Galloway waved a hand, and said gently:

"Come in, Mr. Dawlish, come in. I've been expecting you."

CHAPTER THREE

A FRIENDLY POLICEMAN

The little man closed the door, and left Dawlish alone with Galloway.

"So you've been expecting me," Dawlish murmured.

"Indeed I have. Allow me to congratulate you. A great number of people put themselves out to scrape acquaintance with me. Rarely is it done as skilfully as you contrived it today."

"Oh," said Dawlish, blankly.

"I do ask you, Mr. Dawlish, not to be disheartened," went on Galloway, gaily. "After all, I am so used to these things; you must not feel badly because I have found out so quickly. It would have been unkind to allow you to think that I was taken in. Don't you agree?"

"Oh, most unkind," admitted Dawlish.

"Mr. Dawlish, I am harassed day after day by appeals for charity. Will you allow me to guess why you have come?"

"By all means," murmured Dawlish.

"I imagine that you served throughout the war, probably with distinction. You now find yourself with too small an income to live the life to which you have become accustomed.

You probably represent a number of gentlemen placed in the same position as yourself. You have a company that will make a fortune, if *only* you can find sufficient capital to start it. Mind you, I investigate every proposition. After all, some might be practical."

Dawlish lit a cigarette, and contemplated him in silence. There was something likable about Galloway.

"Perhaps I should add that meeting your wife—a most astute move that, on your part—makes me even more likely to be amenable to any suggestion you have in mind," murmured Galloway.

Dawlish stared—and then laughed with sheer enjoyment.

He pulled himself up. "You have the nerve of Old Harry, you know."

Galloway looked thunderstruck.

"Mr. Dawlish, that is *not* an opening I would recommend for someone who requires my goodwill. I have not much time to spare this evening."

"I'm almost sorry to have to say so, but you're wrong."

"Wrong?" Galloway looked dumbfounded.

"Hopelessly wrong. I don't want you to finance a wild-cat-scheme for me. In the course of time there might be matters worth discussing with you, but I haven't called on any business matter now—but on something which concerns you very closely indeed."

"And may I ask in what way?" asked Galloway. His hand was hovering about a handbell, a miniature maiden of shameless nakedness.

"And summon your secretary by all means," invited Dawlish. "Bring your chauffeur in, too. I've a feeling that you are going to need them."

Galloway snapped, "Will you tell me what you want?"

"Yes. To tell you that the police will soon be coming to see you," said Dawlish.

He did not know why he introduced the subject that way. Certainly he had not dreamed of the effect of his words. Galloway jumped to his feet, gripping the bell. As it was ringing the door opened, and Galloway cried:

"Abbott, show Mr. Dawlish out. I am not at home to him in future. To come here threatening me—blackmail, that's what you're trying, is it? Get out, Dawlish! If you or your wife so much as try to speak me again, I'll summon the police. Out with him, Abbott!"

Now, Abbott was a small man.

He stood looking up at Dawlish, and, as a chucker-out where a man like Dawlish was concerned, Abbott's inadequacy was pathetic.

"This way, Mr. Dawlish," he said, mustering courage.

"Not for a moment," said Dawlish, without getting up. "Sit down, Galloway."

"I insist—"

"Oh, don't be such a peacock!" snapped Dawlish. "I came to tell you that I stopped someone putting strychnine in your tea. The police know about it." He got out of his chair in a single movement and went to the door. "Good-bye," he said, and went into the outer room.

There was a moment of utter silence. Then:

"Dawlish!" cried Galloway.

"Mr. Dawlish!" called Abbott, running after him.

"Dawlish, just a moment!" gasped Galloway, reaching the door breathlessly. "Are you serious?"

"I am," said Dawlish, pausing.

"I—I am really sorry, Mr. Dawlish. Please come and give me more information. I will make handsome amends."

Dawlish stood firm.

"I saw someone drop powder into your milk and sugar. That explains my accidental fall. I took the sugar out of the kitchen and had it analysed. It contained a lethal dose of strychnine. The analyst, naturally, has told the police. I thought it neighbourly to warn you."

Galloway stared at him, speechless. Abbott had backed away. For the first time Dawlish felt sorry for Galloway, who seemed deflated. That he was frightened was only too clear.

Then Galloway said a strange thing.

"So they have followed me here, Abbott."

Dawlish made no comment. Abbott uttered a distressed sound. Galloway went to a chair and sat down. His forehead was wet with sweat.

"I don't think I need stay," said Dawlish.

"Please wait a moment," implored Galloway. "It is a great shock."

Dawlish watched him speculatively. The man was clever; he was gaining time, preparing to make a statement to explain away the oddness of his words.

"You are very good," said Galloway. "Can I presume on your friendliness further, Mr. Dawlish? Do not tell the police that I was foolish enough to say that I had been followed here."

"Why did you say it?" asked Dawlish.

"Because it appears to be true. Rich men make enemies, Mr. Dawlish. I am anxious, most anxious, not to have it known that threats have been made against my life."

"This wasn't a threat, it was an attempt to murder you."

Galloway dabbed his neck. "I know. But I have good reasons for wishing to keep the full gravity of it from the police. At least give me time to see the police and afterwards to tell you why I am so very anxious that this should not become known."

"They will know about the strychnine," said Dawlish.

"Yes, yes. Now that I have been warned, I can deal with that. *Give* me until early evening."

"All right," said Dawlish.

"I cannot say how grateful I am," repeated Galloway, humbly. "I feel that I have been singularly fortunate in meeting you. And your alertness has saved my life. I shall not forget that, Mr. Dawlish."

Galloway got up and wrung his hand. Abbott showed him out.

Superintendent Longstaffe, of the Highsea Police, was well liked. He was a friendly man. He was tall and running to fat, he had a genial smile and a pleasant voice, and he scoffed at the suggestion that there was anything sinister in his occupation. Police work was certainly not sinister in Highsea. Occasionally a body was washed up on the foreshore, and twice that year there had been fatal falls from the cliffs, but such things could happen at any seaside resort. Burglaries were few and petty crime was not particularly prevalent.

In his office that afternoon he was working on arrangements for a Police Fancy Dress Carnival to be held late in the following month, when the telephone rang.

"Longstaffe speaking," he said, in a husky voice.

"I've a Mr. Morrison on the line, sir. He's from Taylor's, the chemist's in Marine Parade. He insists on speaking to you personally, and he seems rather agitated, sir."

"Then I'd better see if I can calm him down," said Longstaffe. "Put him through."

After a pause, Morrison spoke hurriedly. "Is that the Superintendent?"

"What can I do for you, Mr. Morrison?"

"It is a terrible thing," said Morrison. "Someone has put strychnine on the sugar!"

"What's that?" ejaculated Longstaffe.

"I tell you I have it in front of me, I have analysed it carefully and there is no possibility of a mistake," cried Morrison. "There is enough to kill a dozen people. It—"

"Now don't worry about it," said Longstaffe—"don't worry, Mr. Morrison. I will be round to see you in ten minutes." He pressed a bell-push in his desk, and the door opened immediately. A curly-headed, youthful-looking man in a ginger suit looked in.

"Yes, skipper?"

"We're going out," said Longstaffe. "Someone's been putting poison in someone else's sugar."

"I suppose you're serious," said Detective-Inspector Harry May.

"I am. Take the car round at once, will you?"

"Right-ho!" exclaimed Harry May. He looked delighted. "I hope it isn't a mistake."

"Bloodthirsty young devil," growled Longstaffe.

Harry May was forty, but he looked little more than twenty-five. He was a London man and had been with the Scotland Yard C.I.D. before being smitten with tuberculosis. He was ordered twelve months in a Highsea sanatorium, told that Highsea was the right place for him to live, and, when he was given a clear medical certificate, taken on to the force. He and Longstaffe worked well together.

Marine Parade was only a quarter of a mile away. Longstaffe opened the door of the car as May pulled up outside the chemist's shop, and soon the two policemen were standing behind the glass partition which separated the dispensary from the shop itself. In front of Morrison were the sugar knobs, all the paraphernalia of his profession, and a sheet of paper on which he had carefully recorded his findings. The quick response of the police appeared to have surprised him, and he was still nervous although positive that he was right.

"All the same, I think you ought to get someone else to check my findings, Superintendent." He peered up into Longstaffe's face.

"You're quite right," said Longstaffe. "Take some of this to Dr. Anderson, Inspector, and ask him if he can test it immediately, will you?"

"But I am quite sure he will confirm my analysis," declared Morrison.

"I'm sure, too," Longstaffe said, soothingly. May had already packed some of the sugar into a small box, and was on his way.

"Is there a room where we can sit down and talk without being overheard?" Longstaffe asked, and was taken to a small room behind the shop. There, Morrison poured out his story, which included an excellent description of Dawlish.

"Dawlish," mused Longstaffe. "The name's familiar." When Morrison had finished he put in a call to the Marine Hotel. This man Dawlish, he reflected, had his wits about him and would not have asked for a telephone call unless he had a good reason.

Longstaffe had to hold on for some time. Morrison fidgeted. Then a woman's voice came, and Longstaffe frowned.

"This is Mrs. Dawlish," the woman began.

"I am Superintendent Longstaffe of the Highsea Police, and I want particularly to speak to Mr. Dawlish," said Longstaffe.

"And he wants to talk to you," declared Felicity; "he's engaged for a few minutes, Superintendent, but I think he'll be in his room within a quarter of an hour."

"I'll come and see him," said Longstaffe. "Thank you."

He went outside and strolled up and down, while he waited

for May. May would not wait to hear Dr. Anderson's findings but would hurry back, eager to miss nothing. As he waited, Longstaffe pondered over the name Dawlish. He thought he knew now why it was so familiar. If he remembered rightly, the 'Dawlish' who had featured in several sensational spy episodes during the war was a colossus of a man, something like this fellow whom Morrison had described.

Harry May might know him . . .

May drew up outside Taylor's shop, and Longstaffe joined him.

"Don't drive off yet," said Longstaffe; "I want to give the fellow a few more minutes."

"What fellow?"

"The man who brought the sugar to Morrison," said Longstaffe. "A man named Dawlish. Morrison says that he's about six feet five and broad with it, and—"

"Great Scott!" exclaimed Harry May. "It can't be!"

"Can't be what?"

"*That* Dawlish. Pat Dawlish." May broke into a broad smile. "If it is, we're in for some fun, skipper! You've read about him, haven't you?"

"Vaguely."

"There isn't anything vague about Dawlish," declared May, confidently. "I met him several times before the war. He was mixed up in several queer shows, you know, before he was taken over by Intelligence Department, and he created one or two sensations when he was there. He's an astonishing fellow. You know Bill Trivett of the Yard, don't you?"

"Yes."

"Trivett has a tremendously high opinion of Dawlish," May told him. "He thinks that Dawlish has a natural bent for detection."

"Is he a meddler?" demanded Longstaffe.

"Oh, lord, no! Trivett has actually had to persuade him to help in some cases."

"This Dawlish seems to know his way about," said Longstaffe. "I'll ring him again from the kiosk over there," he added. "You drive up to the hotel, and make sure he doesn't leave."

Longstaffe strolled across the road to a telephone kiosk. This time he had no difficulty in getting Dawlish.

"I believe you wanted me to ring you," Longstaffe said.

"Yes," said Dawlish. "You're very good to do it my way. Thanks. However, the emergency is past. Can you spare me half an hour here?"

"Yes, at once."

"I'll be in my room," promised Dawlish.

Longstaffe was recognized at once by the hotel staff. The receptionist looked startled when he asked for Dawlish.

"He's in Room 55," she said. "Shall I tell him you want to see him down here?"

"No, he's expecting me," said Longstaffe.

As a result of his visit, rumour began to spread through the Marine Hotel.

Dawlish and Felicity were sitting in their room, and Longstaffe and May were listening to his story.

Longstaffe sized up the big man.

There was certainly some justification for May's glowing account. Dawlish's eyes were shrewd and steady. He told his story with a minimum of effort, yet drew a vivid word-picture—omitting what Galloway did not want known.

Dawlish raised his hands.

"And that's that. I'm pretty sure that it was an attempt to murder Galloway, and it was neatly done. I'm sorry to have to unload this on to you, Superintendent."

"Well, it's my job," said Longstaffe. "You seem to be able to smell these things out, Mr. Dawlish."

Felicity stirred.

"I didn't smell this one out," said Dawlish. "Galloway recently floated a company which went broke. *Hedshire Estates.*" Longstaffe nodded. "He didn't do anything illegal, but he made me lose eleven thousand pounds. I invested in his company on the best advice."

"Do you mean that you came here to see him?"

"Yes," said Dawlish. "I wanted to size the little beggar up. My wife insisted," he added, with an owlish look at Felicity. "Didn't you, darling?"

"I wish I'd never thought of it," declared Felicity.

"What did you think of doing?" asked Longstaffe.

Dawlish grinned. "I thought I'd wait for a dark night and get him in a corner and scare the life and eleven thousand pounds out of him," he declared. "That's the kind of man I am—ask my wife."

"Sweetheart," cooed Felicity, "you are in your most winsome mood today, aren't you?"

"Well, the truth will prevail," said Dawlish, gravely.

"Be serious for a moment, will you?" asked Longstaffe. "Why did you come?"

"As I say, to find out what I could about Galloway. Scotland Yard assured me that everything he did was strictly legal. The fact remains that he got away with a lot of money—nearly a quarter of a million, altogether. I suspected that he fixed it nicely. I was sore. We were due for a holiday, and Trivett of the Yard mentioned that Galloway was down in Highsea, or on his way. We found he was due to arrive today, and thought it would be a good idea to precede him. After all," went on Dawlish, owlishly, "he might be a bad man."

"And you don't like bad men," said Longstaffe, ironically.

"No more than you do," admitted Dawlish. "And if I could find out that Galloway is as bad as I think he is—"

"You'd come to me immediately," said Longstaffe.

"Exactly."

"I wonder. Will you be here for the next half-hour or so?"

"At your service until seven-thirty," said Dawlish, "and it's now a little after six. We've had an eventful hour or two since Galloway arrived at half past three!"

Longstaffe and May laughed, and went out. As the door closed on them Felicity got off the bed and, set-faced, approached Dawlish threateningly, and began to tell him exactly what she thought of him . . .

CHAPTER FOUR

A VISITOR

"But, darling," protested Dawlish, "I promised Galloway—"

"I don't care what you promised Galloway," stormed Felicity; "you ought to have told the police exactly what happened upstairs. Now you've told them a lot of half-truths, they'll probably find out; they'll be annoyed and—and—" She paused for breath.

"Go on," urged Dawlish.

"They'll make an awful nuisance of themselves," said Felicity. "Why on earth did you have to tell them about *us*? How on earth can you think they'll believe you when you say that the only thing you wanted to do was to find out what Galloway was up to? And why did you say you'd get Galloway in a dark corner and squeeze the money out of him? I thought you'd reached the height of idiocy a long time ago, but this—this beats everything!"

Dawlish suddenly lifted her from the floor and held her high. "Say 'sorry.'"

"Pat, put me down!"

"Say—"

"I'm sorry you're such a hopeless fool!"

Dawlish laughed, lowered her, hugged her until she gasped, and then sat in the big easy chair, with her on his knee.

"The interlude is over," he said, more seriously. "I think it was wise to find out how Galloway will defend his decision to keep salient facts from the police," he said. "Only by promising not to tell them what he had said did I earn the right to see him again. Unless I've got him wrong, he will now feel that he has some hold over me—"

"That's exactly what I mean," said Felicity, sitting snugly on his knee and showing no inclination to get off. "You've lied to the police, so Galloway's hand is strengthened."

"Now, look here," protested Dawlish. "Galloway will have to tell me something. He probably won't tell me the truth, but he certainly won't tell the police the truth. What he says to me and what he says to the police can be compared, and we might get something from that. In any case, we can prove that he's lied to one or the other of us. Thus his position will be weakened."

"You *will* tell the police, afterwards?"

"But I thought that was as clear as glass," said Dawlish.

"Well, provided you do, it won't matter so much," conceded Felicity. "Darling, I trust you on most things, but I don't like the look in your eye."

Dawlish laughed. "I couldn't stand by and see the man poisoned, could I? And don't forget I saved his life. I might be able to persuade him to change his ways."

He tried to assess the situation calmly and dispassionately. He was one of several hundred people who had suffered from a slick deal. Galloway had planned and financed the scheme to float a large company to promote the building of garden cities in various parts of England.

Whitehall had approved the scheme, but it went wrong. It

was a business similar to the Government purchase of unsuitable ground for an aerodrome in Scotland during the war.

The company which had made so much money out of the deal was a private one, and Galloway was its managing director.

When Felicity had heard of it she had been deeply depressed. She had by chance met a middle-aged couple who had put most of their limited capital into it, and were now in a desperate plight. There were many others in a similar position. Felicity, characteristically, had worried about them. She had urged Dawlish to come down here, with no very clear idea of what could be done. Certainly she had not bargained for violence.

"Pat," she said, after a long pause, "do you really think you might be able to do something?"

"It seems more likely now than it did a few hours ago," said Dawlish. "I have a glimmering of an idea," he added; "it's—"

Someone tapped at the door.

"Oh, damn!" exclaimed Felicity, jumping off his lap. "Who is it?" she called.

"You will not know me," said a strange voice, and the door opened on the words.

Dawlish got up, staring in surprise at the man who entered.

He was a tall, thin man. The front of his head was bald. He was dressed in clerical grey, and he carried a black stick with a silver top and a pair of soiled pigskin gloves.

"I must apologize for this intrusion," he said.

"Yes," said Dawlish, uncompromisingly.

"But I assure you I have a very good reason for calling."

He took a card from his pocket and held it out.

Dawlish read: JONATHAN WHITE, CHARTERED ACCOUNTANT, 17 HOLLWAY MANSIONS, CHISWICK.

"I represent a number of people who suffered severely in the *Hedshire Estates Corporation.*"

That shook Dawlish.

"How on earth did you know we'd lost on that?" demanded Felicity.

"It was whispered, Mrs. Dawlish." He sat down and mopped his forehead. "The truth is that I came here in the hope of persuading Mr. Galloway to make *some* amends. Imagine my astonishment when I saw *you,* another victim."

"How did you know I was the same Dawlish?"

"I made it my business to inquire. I learned that you had been a substantial shareholder, Mr. Dawlish. How pleased I was when I learned that a gentleman of your known ability might be persuaded to champion the cause of others. When I saw you outside I decided to postpone my visit to Mr. Galloway. It was my intention to intercede with him on behalf of my clients. A personality such as yours would have far better chance of success, because I had no very high hopes. Mr. Galloway is a hard man."

White held his hands together.

"And now, Mr. Dawlish, I come to the crux of my affairs. *Will* you act on behalf of my clients, Mr. Dawlish?"

Dawlish put his head on one side. White waited nervously.

At last Dawlish said, "How many clients have you, Mr. White?"

"Twenty-seven," said White, promptly.

"*How* many?"

"I assure you that I am not exaggerating," said White. "In my pocket I have a list of them—their names and addresses, the sums of money involved *and* a note of the results of the loss. In most cases the results have been grievous, Mr. Dawlish." He took a foolscap envelope out of his pocket and handed it to Dawlish. "There is the list, for your inspection. The correspondence can be seen at my office at any time. It is voluminous. I have *copies* of that correspondence at my hotel room, which you can also see at any time."

Dawlish nodded, and took out the contents of the envelope, a typewritten list of names and addresses, with a column for the sum involved and another for 'remarks'. He glanced at it cursorily. "How did you come to act for so many people, Mr. White?"

"Alas, the answer is simple," declared White, "and the responsibility is mine, I freely and sadly confess it. I was attracted by the syllabus, Mr. Dawlish. I thought, as I am sure you did, that the company offered great promise. I am fortunate to have an extensive clientele. I recommended *Hedshire Estates.* And, to my sorrow, *twenty-seven* were moved to take my advice."

"Did you buy any shares?" asked Dawlish.

"Yes, five hundred," said White, sharply. "But I am not concerned with my own loss. I can ill afford to lose five hundred pounds, but it would not be true to say that it is a serious matter for me. For my clients, especially those of them whose names have been underlined in red, it is a *most* serious matter. It is on their behalf that I am here."

"I see," said Dawlish.

He scanned the names and addresses. White seemed sincere. His manner was against him, but sincerity was the thing that mattered. His, story was not really surprising.

Dawlish handed the paper to Felicity.

"Why didn't you come to see me before?" he asked.

"I felt that it was my duty to make a personal attempt to get help from Mr. Galloway," said White. "I had firmly decided that I should make one approach, and if it failed I should come to see you. I must confess that I was shaken out of my usual calmness when I saw you outside. I was filled with deep, invigorating hope!"

"I see," said Dawlish. "I have met Galloway here, quite by accident. I did not get the impression that he would be easily moved."

"That, I regret to say, is my own impression," admitted White, "yet I still hope, Mr. Dawlish. *Will* you see Mr. Galloway?"

"Yes," promised Dawlish.

White jumped up. "My dear sir, what a relief! I cannot thank you enough!" He seized Dawlish's hand. "The chance of success is slight, but I am sure that it is greater with you in the position of mediator. Will you see him *soon?*"

"Probably," said Dawlish, "but I shall have to wait for a good opportunity."

"Oh, I understand. I shall wait with keen expectation, Mr. Dawlish. You will understand that I shall not tell any of my clients of your most generous gesture. I should hate to raise their hopes. And now I must go. I have detained you long enough already. If you will reverse the card which I gave you, Mr. Dawlish, you will see written on it the name of the hotel in Highsea where I can be found. I shall not stir from that hotel until half past ten tomorrow morning. I shall anticipate a visit from you, if you are able to broach this subject tonight or tomorrow morning. But I shall understand if I do not hear from you. *Good* evening, Mrs. Dawlish. *Good* evening, Mr. Dawlish."

And Mr. Jonathan White bowed himself out.

Felicity raised her hands and dropped them, with a helpless gesture. Dawlish shot her an amused glance as he went to the door, but White was out of sight. Outside the door, however, was the evening paper, and he picked it up.

"What's that?" asked Felicity.

"The paper," said Dawlish. "Outside instead of inside. If the manager catches the porter at that there'll be trouble." He opened the paper.

"Oh, don't read that now," said Felicity. "What did you make of him?"

"I wouldn't like to say," murmured Dawlish.

"Did you believe him?"

"Well, it's all quite plausible," said Dawlish, pointing to the list which she still held in her hands. "What do you feel about it?"

"To tell you the truth, I didn't take to Mr. White."

"I can't say that I did," said Dawlish. "A cold individual. Somehow it didn't seem in character."

"But if his long-standing clients have lost money, he would probably do the best he could for them."

"Yes," admitted Dawlish. "I suppose he's greatly interested in restoring his reputation. Don't you think that's about it?"

"I suppose so," agreed Felicity.

Dawlish smiled. "We both feel allergic to Jonathan White," he said lightly. "There's another thing puzzling me at the moment."

"What is it?"

"Where are the police?" asked Dawlish. "They've been with Galloway for a long time."

"They didn't say they'd come to see you again."

"Didn't you expect them too?"

"Yes, I did, rather," admitted Felicity. "I expect they'll come. After all," she went on, sarcastically, "they might have seen that Galloway wasn't happy about your visit. That man Longstaffe isn't a fool. Nor's the other man, who seemed to know you. He's very young for an inspector, isn't he?"

"He's older than he looks."

Dawlish opened the evening paper. His expression changed. He gave all his attention to a paragraph in the newspaper.

In the *Stop Press* was a brief item, marked at the sides with a heavy blue-pencilled cross.

CHAPTER FIVE

NEWS OF SUICIDE

The news item read:

Arthur Milsom, 55 Hillyer Terrace, Harrow, threw himself in front of a train and was killed at Baker Street Station early this afternoon. Milsom was a victim of the Hedshire Estates failure. A. P.

Dawlish looked into Felicity's eyes. She handed him the list which White had left. It was in alphabetical order, and rather more than halfway down was the name of Arthur Milsom. He had invested three thousand five hundred pounds in *Hedshire Estates,* and in the 'remarks' column were the words, '*Reduced to desperate plight.*'

Felicity said slowly, "I should have felt dreadful if you'd refused to do anything, Pat."

"Yes," said Dawlish. "Your first reaction was the right one, too. Well, I suppose we'll have to wait until we know the police have gone before we tackle Galloway."

"Will you tell him about that?" asked Felicity.

"I'll see how the land lies," said Dawlish.

On his words there was a tap at the door, and Longstaffe came in. He was looking very pleased with himself, but he assured Dawlish that he had discovered nothing except that Galloway had received a very severe shock. Galloway had told him, that he had no idea that anyone wanted to kill him. He appealed for police protection and had even talked of leaving Highsea next morning.

Longstaffe seemed pleased because Galloway was so upset. It transpired that several people in Highsea had been victimized by the *Hedshire Estates* failure, and that Galloway was not well liked by Longstaffe. It was surprising how much Longstaffe knew about him. He had missed very little. Galloway had started out as a small shopkeeper; he had built a garage, bought a fleet of coaches, and gradually extended his influence until he was now several times a millionaire, although he was only just turned fifty.

"Can I help at all?" asked Dawlish.

"You can keep your eyes open, if you will. I am arranging for a man to watch Galloway's suite, and for another to be on duty in the lounge. No one will know that he's one of us. His name's Carter, a young, good-looking fellow, and he will probably have a girl with him. His fianceé. Pretty kid, with red hair."

"Thanks," said Dawlish.

"That's all right. Then I shall look through the doctor's report on the sugar," said Longstaffe, and added reassuringly: "I think I can promise you that we won't fall down on the job, Mr. Dawlish. I wish you could recognize the hand that dropped the powder."

"So do I," said Dawlish.

"Anything else worth telling me about?" asked Longstaffe.

There was something in the way he looked as he put the question which made Dawlish wary.

Dawlish showed him the newspaper first, and then told

the story of White's visit. Longstaffe was affected most by the news of the suicide.

"I hope Galloway knows he's responsible for this," said Longstaffe, and then shrugged his shoulders. "Still, I mustn't get this thing out of perspective, must I? This kind of tragedy does occur from time to time; it's hardly Galloway's fault. It's one of the results of making money without being overscrupulous." He looked thoughtful. "I suppose Galloway did know that the land was worthless?"

"I don't know," said Dawlish. "That sort of thing isn't in my line. Give me murder! I do know a little about that."

Longstaffe ignored his flippancy.

"Are you going to talk to him about White's visit?" he asked.

"I'll see how the land lies," said Dawlish. "I think he'd better have his dinner first."

Longstaffe laughed. "I needn't give you any tips, I can see. He's having dinner in his room, by the way. What did you make of the secretary?"

"Cold-blooded little customer," said Dawlish.

"That about sums him up. Well, keep in touch," added Longstaffe, and went out.

It was then nearly a quarter past seven, and Felicity had not changed for dinner. She did so while Dawlish sat on the bed and pondered over the general situation.

"A penny for them," said Felicity, putting the finishing touches to her make-up.

"The tilt of your chin," said Dawlish.

"Sweet, but untrue," said Felicity. "I'm hungry, darling. Are you?"

"Yes," said Dawlish. "Highsea air for hearty appetites. The Town Council might give me a fiver for that slogan!"

They went downstairs, and attracted much attention in the lounge, where they had a sherry before going in to dinner.

Dawlish was preoccupied during the meal.

Who had marked the news item in blue pencil? Who else could have known that he was interested in *Hedshire Estates?* No one, so far as he knew, was aware of it except the police and White. Someone who knew had thought it worth while to place the paper there furtively. The fact that it was outside, not tucked beneath the door, was curious.

"Another penny," offered Felicity.

"The newspaper," said Dawlish. "Not worth the money! Coffee here, or in the lounge?"

"The lounge, I think, if it isn't too crowded."

It was then half past eight. They found empty chairs by the window and, still furtively watched by many people, sat and chatted over coffee. Dawlish was startled when a page-boy came up and said:

"Mr. Dawlish, please."

"Oh, hallo. What is it?"

"Wanted on the telephone, sir," said the boy. "Box 7."

"Thanks." Dawlish went off, expecting to hear from Longstaffe.

Instead, he heard a voice which was most deferential. Could Mr. Dawlish spare Mr. Galloway a few minutes in his suite?

"Oh, yes," said Dawlish.

"That is very good of you, sir," said Galloway's secretary. "I will tell Mr. Galloway to expect you almost at once."

Dawlish went back to the lounge. He suggested that Felicity should amuse herself trying to find out which was Carter and his red-haired young woman. Then he walked up to the first floor.

At the end of the passage sat a heavily-built man whom Dawlish imagined to be Longstaffe's watch-dog. The man nodded in response to his smile. Then the secretary opened the door and immediately led the way into the larger room. Galloway, dressed in a dinner-jacket and smoking a cigar, was sitting at a writing-table.

"There are several things I think we might discuss with advantage," began Galloway, "but before we do, Mr. Dawlish, I want to say again how much I am in your debt. The police, as you no doubt know, confirmed what you told me. But for your prompt action, I should be dead. I cannot think of any way in which I can repay my debt, Mr. Dawlish."

Dawlish waved a hand.

The room was pleasantly warm. A table-lamp, shining near Galloway's side, showed up his slight double chin and his sleepy brown eyes. It was curious, thought Dawlish, that he had not previously noticed those brown eyes before. Galloway looked drowsy; he seemed to have shaken off the effect of the attempt to murder him.

"Well, Mr. Dawlish," said Galloway, "I formed a good impression of Wagstaffe."

"Longstaffe," corrected Dawlish.

"Oh, to be sure—Longstaffe. I am convinced that the police now think that I am shocked, even a little nervous, but that I had no earlier intimation of the possibility of such violence."

"Whereas you most certainly had."

"I made that obvious to you this afternoon," said Galloway, calmly. "I have been living so close to death for so long that I am inured to danger. I had hoped to have some rest in Highsea. This constant watchfulness is wearing to the nerves. However, I am prepared to face it as I have faced it for years. And you, Mr. Dawlish, are not unused to danger, I believe."

Dawlish said, "I served through the war."

"After your call this afternoon, I made some inquiries. I now know quite a lot about your activities. I expect you know what the world knows about me. I am a very rich man. I have made enemies. One of those enemies, to my distress, is a close personal friend, and has turned against me. I hope that I shall be able to find him and make him see my point of view. However, until I succeed I must confess that a state of war exists between us. I do not want to harm my friend; I certainly do not want him to be arrested and charged with uttering threats or trying to commit murder. I know that my friend has suffered much provocation, and he is completely in the hands of other people who have designs *only* on my money."

"I see," said Dawlish.

"I repeat, I am very anxious indeed not to set the police on my friend." He paused. "I hope that you agree with my policy, Mr. Dawlish."

Dawlish said, "I don't know all the circumstances."

"I do not think I can go into further detail," Galloway said, "except, of course, I can give you the name of my friend. A Mr. Giles Lancing, of whom you may have heard."

"The name doesn't sound familiar," said Dawlish.

"He figured in some sensational financial speculations before the war," said Galloway, "when he was the managing director of the Lancing Trust. Unfortunately he failed and had to file a petition in bankruptcy. I am sure that a little research would bring him to your mind."

"Possibly," said Dawlish.

"He went abroad," continued Galloway, "and I lost touch with him. Then I received threatening letters and threats by telephone, and gradually I came to realize that Lancing was behind them all. I found that he was in the hands of unscrupulous men. My deep regard for him—and I may say, also, my deep regard for his daughter—made me do what I have done."

"Where is his daughter?" asked Dawlish.

"She is now in London," Galloway told him. "She was left destitute. For a while she lived as my guest, but she is an independent young woman, and now prefers to earn her own living. She has a flat in Kensington and, I believe, is doing fairly well. I am very fond of her, Mr. Dawlish, as fond of her as I would be of my own daughter. She does provide a very strong motive for my restraint."

After a pause, Dawlish said, gravely, "It is a most remarkable story, Mr. Galloway."

"I agree with you," said Galloway, "but then, a man of your varied experience must have been told many remarkable stories, and will be able to believe this, strange though it may seem."

"Oh, yes, I've heard plenty," said Dawlish, non-committally. "I think—"

He stopped, for there was a sudden cry outside. A woman was saying something which he could not catch. Galloway started. The secretary's voice followed, then the deep rumbling tones of another man—the watch-dog, Dawlish fancied. Galloway was staring fixedly towards the door.

"*I must see him!*" the woman cried.

Galloway snapped his fingers. "Why does Abbott allow me to be disturbed like this?" The door burst open and a girl rushed wildly into the room.

Two things struck Dawlish at once. She was easy to look at, and in great distress. She was in her early twenties, tall, with dark, unruly hair, and she stood in front of Galloway, breathing heavily.

Abbott was also breathing hard. He stood in the doorway, with the policeman just behind him.

"What does this mean, Abbott?" snapped Galloway. "I gave you instructions that I must not be disturbed. Young lady, if you care to make an appointment, I will be happy to see you tomorrow."

"No," she said, "I'm going to see you now."

"If the young woman is making a nuisance of herself, I will instruct her to leave," said Longstaffe's man.

Galloway hesitated. Dawlish went to the girl's side, smiling. She looked at him in surprise. He led her to his chair, and she sat down, still bewildered. Galloway frowned. The policeman looked dumbfounded.

Dawlish said, "One of the things you can do for me is to see her now, Mr. Galloway."

"Oh," said Galloway, after a long pause. "Yes, I see. All right, constable. Wait outside, Abbott." When the door was closed he turned and looked at Dawlish. He was angry, but trying to conceal it.

"Is the matter private?" he asked the girl.

"I don't think it can be as private as all that," Dawlish answered for her, and Galloway shot him another angry look. "What is the trouble, Miss—"

"My name is Kingham," said the caller.

"I do not think we are acquainted," Galloway said, absurdly. "What is it you want, Miss Kingham?"

The girl hesitated.

"Well?" snapped Galloway.

"I—I want to see you about my father," the girl said, at last. "You've ruined him! He put all his money into *Hedshire Estates*. He doesn't know which way to turn, and you're responsible."

Galloway said: "I am afraid there is a misunderstanding. I am not responsible for the failure of the *Hedshire Estates* business."

She recoiled. "You know that's not true."

"I won't have people bursting into my rooms and making

ridiculous assertions!" snapped Galloway. "What do you think I am? If a company fails, am I to be blamed for it? I was not even concerned with that company; it was handled by foolish men who made fools of others. Your father got what he deserved."

Galloway found Dawlish watching him steadily. He averted his gaze. He raised a hand, and said more mildly:

"Naturally, I am sorry for your distress, but there is nothing I can do. I am afraid that is final."

She was fighting to keep her self-control. Her eyes were blazing. Galloway looked anxiously towards the door. Dawlish said nothing, but when the girl shot a quick glance towards him, he smiled reassuringly.

She snatched a newspaper cutting from her handbag. "Do you see what you've done already? Do you want others to do the same thing?"

Galloway picked up the cutting.

Dawlish saw that it was the *Stop Press* of the *Evening News*. He saw Galloway's eyes narrow. He schooled himself, and spoke much more gently.

"If I were responsible for such a thing as this, Miss Kingham, then it would indeed lie heavy on my conscience. If you had any knowledge of the way such matters are done, you would understand that I am not responsible. I do not blame you, but there is *nothing* I can do. Would you like me to send you home in my car?"

The girl turned to Dawlish.

"Can't you make him do something?"

"Now that is enough!" snapped Galloway, losing his temper again. "You are impertinent. Go away."

She faced him again. "If anything happens to my father," she began, "I shall never forgive you, and—"

"Don't talk nonsense!" snapped Galloway.

Galloway obviously did not dream of what was going to happen. She swung her hand and struck him across the face. He staggered sideways and fell with a thump.

Dawlish said, "You'd better go, Miss Kingham, and—"

Then Galloway got up.

He dusted himself down. Dawlish did not realize what he was going to do.

Galloway flung himself at the girl.

He struck her across the face with a resounding blow which sent her flying, leapt again and struck her on the arm. She gasped and stumbled. Galloway's eyes were blazing, his lips were drawn back. He made a horrible picture, with his hands clenched and raised, and he drew back his foot, as if to kick her.

Dawlish shot out a hand.

The force of his blow was enough to send Galloway rocking back on his heels. The girl picked herself up. Dawlish took her arm, and then as Galloway began to scramble to his feet, he took the man by the scruff of the neck and held him at arm's length.

"That wasn't pretty," he said. "Apologies are called for. Be quick, Galloway."

CHAPTER SIX

GALLOWAY APOLOGIZES

Galloway tried to free himself, but quickly gave up the struggle. The girl was pale now, and there was a tiny trickle of blood at the corner of her lips.

"I'll be damned if I'll apologize! She asked for it. She can think herself lucky if I don't make a charge."

Dawlish murmured: "You owe me a little, don't you?"

Galloway stiffened and stared at Dawlish. The words had shocked him. Opposition was a new, unpleasant experience.

The girl pulled herself free from Dawlish and turned miserably towards the door.

"Don't go," said Dawlish. She turned and looked at him dully. "Now, Galloway," Dawlish continued, as if he were speaking to a child.

Galloway averted his eyes.

"I—I am sorry; indeed I am. I should not have lost my temper like that."

"Thank—thank you," the girl said, and turned again.

"Miss Kingham," said Dawlish, "I want you to promise me one thing. Don't mention this episode to anyone. Explain that you fell and hurt your face. It wouldn't be wise for you to tell the truth."

Galloway perked up. "No, indeed it wouldn't." He looked at Dawlish as if he understood now what Dawlish had been driving at. "May I have your assurance, Miss Kingham?"

"Yes," she said. Her spirit had quite gone.

"What is your address?" asked Dawlish.

"I live in Sea Terrace," she said, and then she quickened her pace and went out.

Galloway shrugged his coat into position.

"That was most discreet of you," he admitted, with a nod of satisfaction. "I am glad you thought of it, Dawlish. I do not want to be involved in a police-court case at this moment. I am glad you were here."

"Good," said Dawlish, heavily. "I'm glad, too. Now, supposing you sit down and write a cheque for one thousand pounds, made payable to Miss Kingham."

Galloway jumped. "*What?* You must be mad!"

"Oh, not mad at all," said Dawlish. "You see, Galloway, you are in a very difficult position. I was the only witness to what happened. If I cared to say that you made an unprovoked attack on Miss Kingham, you would most certainly be sent to prison for two months. The defence would cost you money. So the quickest and cheapest way out of it is to make a gift of one thousand pounds to Miss Kingham."

"So you *are* blackmailing me," breathed Galloway.

"No, I'm simply pointing out a wise course of action," said Dawlish. "That is why I wanted Miss Kingham not to speak of this to anyone else. I should hate a third party to hear a different version of the story."

Galloway went to the writing-table, and leaned against it. He was smiling, but looked wary.

"Now I see your little game," he said. "It's clever, Dawlish, but I am used to dealing with people like you. You arranged for Miss Kingham's visit. But I shall not pay you one penny, Dawlish. I shall call your bluff. I am grateful to you, personally, and I would have been glad to reward you. But blackmail, no. Haven't you forgotten that there is a policeman outside?"

Dawlish laughed. "No. You've forgotten that I can tell the police your real reaction to the attempt to murder you."

"I shall deny it. Abbott will also deny it. I am afraid *that* won't work, Dawlish. Good night."

Dawlish took out his cigarette-case.

"Unless I take a cheque for one thousand pounds with me, I shall go straight to Superintendent Longstaffe and lay a charge of assault against you."

"Oh, no. You won't go that far."

"Think again," said Dawlish. "I shall also tell the police that you went berserk after Miss Kingham had shown you the little notice in the paper. I shall also tell the Press the full story. They will write it up in such a fashion that it will look as if you admitted, by your anger, to being responsible for the *Hedshire Estates* disaster."

Galloway had wilted. "This is criminal! I won't be blackmailed!"

"It isn't blackmail," said Dawlish. "It's more like whitemail. Personally, I don't mind what you do. I would like to take a cheque to Miss Kingham's father, but I'm much more interested in seeing what the newspapers would make of tonight's episode."

"I shall not easily forgive this," said Galloway.

"I haven't easily forgiven you for the way you acted just now," said Dawlish. "The other things were trivial compared with this. The way you lost your temper was remarkable. It would interest pathologists. What is it to be—the whole story to the police and Press, or a cheque for one thousand pounds?"

Galloway slowly turned, took a cheque-book from his pocket, and began to write. After the word 'Pay' he began 'Patrick . . .'

"Tear that one up," said Dawlish. "Miss Kingham's the name."

"Need you pretend?" snapped Galloway.

"I'm not pretending."

Galloway tore the cheque up and wrote another.

"Now open it," said Dawlish. "Make it payable over the counter. I shall arrange for Miss Kingham to be at the bank a little after ten o'clock in the morning. And I shall be at your side when you are telephoning your bankers and authorizing them to pay it."

Galloway paused, but finished as instructed. Then he tore the cheque out of the book and flung it at Dawlish.

"You could be more gracious," remarked Dawlish. He put the cheque in his pocket. "I think we are going to see a lot of each other, Galloway. You did say that you had learned a little of what I did before the war, didn't you?"

"I always suspected you were a cheap rogue," sneered Galloway. "One day *I'll* tell the newspapers—"

"Hush!" chided Dawlish. "Be sensible. You have many worries—including the identity of the man who tried to poison you. He's Lancing, you suggest. I wonder. Shall I tell you something of great interest, Galloway?"

"Get out!"

"I'm going soon," Dawlish said, "but this is really of great interest. I lost a large sum in *Hedshire Estates*."

Galloway gasped, "*You* did!"

"Yes. One of the many fools, you see. Now that doesn't make me very well disposed towards you. Still, I've made a start."

"What do you mean, a start?"

Dawlish smiled. "The Kinghams weren't the only people who

suffered, were they? The poor fellow who was driven to suicide had a wife no doubt, and possibly children. You might ponder over the wisdom of making some amends to them. You're a wealthy man, you can well afford it."

"You'll never get another penny out of me!"

"That depends on how you behave," said Dawlish.

He went out of the room so quickly that Galloway was left staring at the open door.

For some seconds Galloway stood rigid. Then Abbott appeared in the doorway, looking scared. Galloway began to tell him what manner of fool he was. Abbott endured that, white-faced, until Galloway grew hoarse. He flung himself into a chair, and waved Abbott away.

Meanwhile, Dawlish was walking along the moonlit streets, with Felicity. He was obviously delighted with himself.

They paused at the end of a road leading off the promenade.

"I think this is Sea Terrace," said Dawlish.

They had looked in the telephone directory and found that a Kenneth Kingham lived at 17 Sea Terrace.

He opened the gate of the small house, standing in its own grounds. The light was on in the front room, and the curtains were drawn. They could hear the sound of voices, but it was not until they were close to the window that Dawlish recognized one voice. He pulled up, gripping Felicity's arm.

"What is it?" Felicity asked, in alarm.

Dawlish said in a strained voice: "That voice. Listen."

A man was saying: "You understand, my dear sir, that I am taking a *very* grave risk, but I feel a sense of responsibility. I wish that I could do more than I have already done."

Felicity whispered, "That's White!"

"Who is supposed to be sitting by the telephone, waiting to hear from me," said Dawlish.

"What on earth is he doing?"

"Buying Kingham's worthless shares in *Hedshire Estates,* I fancy."

"But that's fantastic!"

"Yes. Still, what other explanation can there be?"

"What are you going to do?"

"I think it might be wise to follow Mr. White," said Dawlish. "You'd better take the cheque to the Kinghams and tell them what happened. White may have other calls to make. Find out exactly what he has offered, won't you, and get the full story as clearly as you can."

"But—" began Felicity.

"We can't lose time," Dawlish said. "He's coming out."

A door opened. Dawlish saw a three-foot wall which divided the Kinghams' house from that next door. He took Felicity by the waist and lifted her over, then stepped over himself. They hid in the porch as White left the house.

Dawlish pushed the cheque into Felicity's hand and kissed her ear.

Then he walked quickly to the street, and hurried after White.

White turned right towards the promenade. Dawlish quickened his step and reached the corner as the other man crossed the road. Apparently he was not returning to his hotel.

White did not look round.

Dawlish found it easy to keep within comfortable distance of him, and his thoughts began to roam. He had acted on impulse with Galloway, but did not think that any harm had been done. Galloway undoubtedly wished he had not told that story about Lancing. There might be a germ of truth in it, but it was certainly not the real explanation of Galloway's reluctance to tell the police the whole truth. The man was frightened lest the police should learn why the attempt had been made to murder him.

There was one consoling feature: the thousand pounds for the Kinghams.

That Galloway had a guilty conscience was evident.

White was striding along, without looking round, fifty yards in front of Dawlish, and they had been walking for ten minutes. Not far ahead Dawlish could see the grey shape of the cliffs, rising out of the sea. The moonlight lent them mystery.

What was the truth about White?

The fact that he had presumably bought the shares of the worthless company from Kingham was startling. No sane man would buy worthless stock, and White was certainly not a philanthropist.

Had he bought the stock for his clients?

The road was uphill now, but White's pace did not slacken. There were no other people about.

There was a fork in the road, one leading to the housing estate, the other up the cliff. White went up the cliff.

Dawlish frowned as he tried to remember what houses there were in that direction.

The hill grew steeper. The moonlight shone on several houses, but White passed them. Surely the man was not out for a walk! Dawlish began to feel uneasy. It was possible that White knew who was behind him. This might be a deliberate attempt to mislead him.

Then White turned into the gateway of one of the houses.

Dawlish waited until he had been admitted, then walked quietly up to the house. There was no light at the front of the house, but a yellow glare shone into the garden from one side. He approached it carefully. He could hear voices, but could not distinguish any words.

He went nearer, and found that the curtains were not drawn; he peered in.

White was sitting at a table, opposite an oldish man whose white hair glinted beneath the light. In an easy chair in one corner sat a woman, staring at White open-mouthed. The man, too, seemed astonished by what White was saying. White seemed to talk ceaselessly for five minutes, and then drew a cheque-book from his pocket.

The old man, looking dazed, got up and went to a pedestal-desk which stood in the window. He unlocked a drawer, and took out the original prospectus of *Hedshire Estates*. There was a thin book, too, in a blue cover—a shareholder's book. White examined it. Then he drew a cheque and handed it to the man.

His hand was gripped tightly. The man seemed almost in tears. The woman jumped up, and for the first time Dawlish heard a word. "I must get you some tea!"

White obviously refused, and stood up.

Dawlish hurried down the path, turned towards the town, and waited in the shadows. White reappeared, then turned towards the town, and passed Dawlish with an easy stride.

From here Dawlish could see the cliffs and the path much more clearly. Coming up, he had not realized how steep the cliffs were, but now he could see the sheer drop, and hear the sea lapping against the rocks below. White kept to the far side of the road. So did Dawlish.

He was quite unprepared for the next development. A small, dark figure suddenly appeared from behind an old brick wall. The figure flung itself at White, and the tall man was taken so much by surprise that he staggered into the road.

Another figure appeared. The men grabbed White's arms, and frog-marched him towards the edge of the cliff.

CHAPTER SEVEN

A CLEAR CASE OF MURDER

White shouted: "Help!"

One of the men moved his free arm and struck the tall man across the face. They reached the opposite pavement. Only a frail railing separated them from the edge of the cliff. There was no doubt at all what they intended to do. White realized it, for he was struggling desperately.

Dawlish reached the nearest man and struck him a blow which made him loosen his hold. Dawlish struck again, driving him towards the road. The man collapsed. White was on the edge of the cliff, his arms waving wildly. The other man kicked at White's legs. Dawlish heard the crunch as his foot landed.

White shrieked and toppled over the edge.

The man turned and ran, leaving his accomplice in the road, while Dawlish darted forward and tried to grab White's legs. He touched his ankle, but could not get a grip.

White disappeared.

Then Dawlish, grabbing at the fence to keep his balance, heard a sound behind him. He glanced round. The man whom he had knocked down was up again, *and striking at him.*

Against Dawlish the man was puny, but Dawlish was off his balance, with the drop yawning in front of him. He dared not let go of the wooden railings. He felt a blow at the back of his knees, and bent involuntarily. His right foot slipped over the edge. He felt the railings giving way under his weight.

The man kicked at him again. *The railings splintered.*

Dawlish fell forward, still gripping them. He did not see his assailant turn and run, convinced that his job was done. Only the cracked railings kept him from falling, and they were gradually breaking. He tried to throw himself backwards, but there was no hope that way.

His right foot was on a tuft of grass, which gave him some foothold. He looked down. There seemed nothing between him and disaster except that tuft of grass. He put his full weight on it. It held him. He leaned backwards, the top of his head level with the cliff edge. The tuft began to loosen; he could feel himself slipping. With agonizing slowness he put out his right arm, over the edge of the cliff, and he gripped another stake which held the railing in position. He eased himself up, gripped the stake more firmly, and then took his life literally in one hand.

He swung his left arm and pulled it round to support his right. For a few seconds he hung on, relying on that single stake. It held firm. He put his whole weight on it, and hauled himself up . . .

He sat on the asphalt pavement, safe, gasping, bemused.

No one had heard White's cries, no one had heard the struggle. He went hot, then cold. He wiped his forehead. At last he stood up. He was a little unsteady.

Slowly he walked across the road.

Farther down the road he could see a red light on a moving vehicle. It was probably a car which had been parked farther down the cliff, and in which the murderers had escaped. If he could get a message to the police quickly, that car might be stopped.

He saw it turn off the promenade and disappear.

By then he was running towards the nearest house. He called out as he reached the gate, and by the time he reached the porch the door was open and a man stood staring at him.

"Telephone, please," gasped Dawlish. "Where is it?"

"In—here," said the man.

Dawlish pushed past him and grabbed the telephone. There was a long pause. Two young girls came out of the front room and stared at him, and a woman was saying, "What is it, George; what on earth's the matter?"

The operator said, "Number, please."

"Police headquarters, quickly," said Dawlish. He asked for Longstaffe.

"He's at his home I think, sir, but I can put you through."

"Hurry, please," pleaded Dawlish.

There was another pause. Then Longstaffe's husky voice came through.

Dawlish said: "A car has just turned off the promenade into one of the roads between the cliffs and Marine Parade. I think it's two turnings before Marine Parade, I can't be sure. There are two men in it. You want them for pushing a man over the cliffs. Call it murder."

"*Murder!*" ejaculated the man behind him.

Dawlish rang off, with a feeling of deep gratitude towards the Highsea policeman. He was surprised to find himself still trembling.

"You—you'd better come and have a drink," said the man. "Marion, don't stand and stare like that, it's rude. Both of you go upstairs and help your mother." He led Dawlish into a pleasantly-furnished room. "I know you must need a drink," he said. "Are you—are you *sure* there has been a murder?"

"A man was pushed over the cliff," Dawlish said. "I saw him go. Not much hope for him, I'm afraid." He took the glass. "I'm afraid I startled you."

"Well, you did, rather. As a matter of fact, you're enough to scare anyone, but I don't think you're as bad as you look."

"Look?" echoed Dawlish, and then caught sight of a mirror.

There was dirt on one side of his face and he had scratched himself a little, so that blood was mixed with the dirt. There was another bleeding scratch above his right eye.

He laughed. "Yes, I do look a wreck."

"My wife's gone upstairs for the first-aid cabinet," said the man. "I wonder if you'd rather tidy up in the bathroom?"

"I would, please," said Dawlish, "but I mustn't stay long."

"No, I understand. You police—" He paused.

Dawlish smiled. "No, I'm not a policeman."

Dawlish went upstairs. In ten minutes he was looking and feeling more himself.

Now that it was all over, he could laugh at his own fears.

As he reached the main promenade, a car turned out of a side road, and he heard his name called.

He looked across the road and saw Inspector May.

"Dawlish!" called May again. "Where did it happen?"

Dawlish told him. Two of the three men with May jumped out of the car and hurried towards the beach. By then two other men had reached the beach and were pushing and pulling at one of the small boats.

"I think you'd better show us just where it happened. Can you find room in the back?"

Dawlish got in. They began the stiff ascent. Soon the light shone on the broken railings. They all got out, and May pulled a face.

"You chose the most dangerous spot," he said.

"I didn't choose it," Dawlish reminded him. He peered over the edge and fancied that he saw a dark patch near the sea. "That looks like White," he said.

"Do you mean to say you know this fellow?"

"Yes. He's the man who called to see me this afternoon," Dawlish said. "Now could I be wrong," he asked, "or is there a thought at the back of your mind that I might have pushed this fellow over?"

"Great Scott, no!" exclaimed May.

Dawlish was sure, however, that the thought had crossed his mind. May drove farther up the hill, to a point where he could shine the headlights nearer to the foot of the cliff. Other lights appeared. Someone down below had a powerful torch. Soon the chug-chug of a motor-boat engine echoed clearly across the water.

"That's a naval cutter," May remarked, "with a searchlight, I hope—yes, there it is."

May called down, making a megaphone of his hands.

"Have you found him?"

"Aye, aye!" came a roar from below.

"Need we stop here?" asked Dawlish.

"You needn't wait, but I'm afraid you'll have to walk back."

"I think I'll do that," said Dawlish.

"You'll go straight to the hotel, won't you?"

"Yes," promised Dawlish.

As he walked down the hill, Dawlish wondered how much to tell Felicity. Not until he was within sight of the floodlit Marine Hotel did he decide, and he did so with a laugh: he would tell her the whole story.

The porters on duty saluted him. He hurried up the stairs, and caught sight of himself in a full-length mirror on the landing. He still looked dirty and dishevelled.

Fooling, he tapped lightly on the door. There was no answer. He tapped again; Felicity had probably heard him approach, and guessed who it was. There was still no answer, and he opened the door, frowning.

The room was empty.

"That's odd," he said aloud. He did not think that Felicity would have stayed at the Kinghams' house so long. It was now nearly ten o'clock, and he had left her at a little after half past eight.

He picked up the telephone as he glanced at the 'K' section of the directory, and gave the Kinghams' number. There was a long pause, before a woman's voice sounded; it was Miss Kingham.

"Good evening," he said. "My name is Dawlish, and we met in Mr. Galloway's rooms this evening. I wonder—"

"Mr. Dawlish! Mrs. Dawlish has been here, we—we just can't say how much we appreciate what you have done. It—it's wonderful!"

"Oh, that's all right," said Dawlish. "Is—"

"I don't know how on earth you managed it," went on Miss Kingham, excitedly. "I am going to London on the eight-ten. I suppose Mrs. Dawlish has told you about the other visitor we had."

"I haven't seen her yet," said Dawlish.

"Do you mean she hasn't got back? She left an hour ago," said the girl, in astonishment.

"She is probably downstairs," Dawlish said, without conviction. "I must have a word with her, Miss Kingham, I'll telephone you later."

He rang off. If Felicity had left the Kinghams' house an hour ago she should have been at the hotel for some time. He had expected her to be waiting for him.

He hurried downstairs with a sinking heart.

"Has my wife come in lately?" he asked the night porter.

"I don't think so, sir," the man said. "I haven't seen her myself—I'll inquire."

"Do, please," said Dawlish.

There was no sign of Felicity. The porter came back, shaking his head.

Dawlish stood looking out of the door, then went out and waited on the porch.

He remembered the way the two men had jumped out of the darkness at White. Had a similar attack been made on Felicity as she had walked from the Kinghams' house?

A car drew up, and to his relief he saw Longstaffe get out.

"Hallo, Mr. Dawlish," he said, "you're the very man I want to see."

"You're the man I want to see, too," said Dawlish, heavily. "My wife has been missing for over an hour."

Longstaffe looked at him sharply.

"What do you mean, missing?"

Dawlish told the whole story quickly. Longstaffe nodded, and went with him into the hall. He used the telephone nearest the door, and gave instructions to police headquarters to make inquiries about Felicity.

Longstaffe came out. "I'm sorry about this, Dawlish," he said, dropping formality. "There are several things I'd like to talk to you about, but if you'd rather be looking for your wife I don't mind waiting until the morning."

"I don't know where to start looking," Dawlish said. "We'd better go upstairs and talk in my room."

As he opened the door Dawlish had an absurd hope that Felicity would be sitting in the room. But she was not there.

Longstaffe sat down. "This must be very worrying. Did you come here expecting something like this, Dawlish?"

"I did not," Dawlish said, emphatically. "It was only a whim which brought us here. I wanted to form my own judgment of Galloway. You know why. What can I tell you?"

"Just what happened tonight?" asked Longstaffe. "I've had a word with May, who tells me that you knew the man who was pushed over the cliff."

"Yes—you remember I told you about White's call?" Longstaffe nodded. "We went to see the Kinghams," Dawlish went on, wondering how much he had better tell the police. Longstaffe's steady gaze convinced him that it would be wise to be wholly frank. He smiled. "We went because Miss Kingham visited Galloway, but you've heard about that, I suppose?"

"Yes, my man told me."

"Well, I worked on Galloway after that," Dawlish said, and told the whole story. Longstaffe did not interrupt.

"Do you know why White wanted to buy these shares?"

"No. But I'm sure he bought them."

"Do you know how much he paid for them?"

"I haven't a notion," Dawlish said, "but his cheque-book should be in his pocket, and I expect he filled in the counter-foils. The Kinghams could tell you, of course."

"I won't worry them just yet," said Longstaffe. "I know the family," he added, and talked for some minutes about them.

"And what is the official police view of my effort to make Galloway cough up?"

"Make?" asked Longstaffe. "I prefer to say that you appealed to his better nature!" He laughed. "You needn't worry about that, Dawlish, but there is one thing I am worried about."

"What's that?"

"You were the only person who saw what happened to White."

"I see," said Dawlish. "Well, I did see what happened to him and I did not throw him over myself! I fancy May will have found traces of the other men by now."

"Possibly," said Longstaffe. "I hope so. White's dead, of course. He broke his neck. I don't want to be difficult, but you do see that I must make every inquiry about it, don't you?"

"Yes," said Dawlish. "Don't mind me."

"I don't want to place any restrictions on your movements," Longstaffe went on, "but I must take all the usual precautions. Will you let me have a few hours' notice if you are going to leave Highsea?"

"Yes, gladly."

"Thanks," said Longstaffe. "Now, naturally, your chief worry is your wife."

Dawlish said, "Did you tell your people to ring through here if there is any news?"

"Yes. They haven't had much time yet, of course."

"I suppose not," said Dawlish. He was striving to repress his anxiety, but it was not easy. "What about the car I warned you about?"

"We didn't find it in Highsea," Longstaffe said, "but a small car, a Ford according to the man who was on patrol duty on the promenade, did turn up West Street about the time you saw this one moving off. Our man saw it start off from the foot of the hill. West Street leads straight into the London Road," added Longstaffe, "and there's a fork which goes to Brighton. Both of those roads were watched. It was probably too late, of course, but if the driver does anything silly, we'll pick him up."

"I see," said Dawlish. "There isn't much chance of him making a fool of himself. And it could have turned off West Street and gone to another part of Highsea."

"Of course."

"It's an odd show," said Dawlish. "I wonder if White was the man who tried to poison Galloway. No, I don't think it was. Difficult to tell, of course, as I only saw his hands."

"What were you going to suggest?" asked Longstaffe.

"I was hoping that we could say that only White and Galloway are concerned," said Dawlish. "If White tried to kill Galloway, Galloway might conceivably have guessed it was he, and taken steps to deal with him. This is the wildest conjecture, of course. I'm not accusing Galloway or his agents of attempted murder."

"Obviously, it's possible," admitted Longstaffe. "What do you make of Galloway?"

"I don't like him at all."

"Nor do I," said Longstaffe, frankly. "Nor, apparently, does someone else! Did Galloway confide in you?"

"He oozed friendliness," Dawlish said. "That made me like him even less. I—"

The telephone-bell rang.

Dawlish was across the room in a flash. "Hallo."

"There's a call for you," said the hotel operator, and after an interminable pause Felicity spoke in a faraway voice.

CHAPTER EIGHT

FELICITY

"Pat, is that you?"

"Oh, my sweet," cried Dawlish, "you've had me on pins for the last couple of hours!"

Felicity sounded woebegone. "Darling, I'm stranded miles from anywhere. I don't even know where I am. It's a little village, but I can't read the name of the exchange. It must be miles from Highsea."

"Leave the receiver off, knock at a door, and find out the name of the village," said Dawlish. "Then I'll come and fetch you."

"I—I'm a bit scared," Felicity said. "I'm afraid someone's watching the kiosk. I—I'm scared stiff."

Dawlish's heart beat fast. "All right, hold on a moment," he said. "Don't ring off." For Felicity to sound like that, she must be scared. He tapped the receiver up and down, and the hotel operator answered. "Hold my caller on, please," said Dawlish, "and then put me on to Inquiries, will you?"

"What do you want to know, sir?"

"The police want to know the number from which my caller is speaking," said Dawlish.

Longstaffe came over and took the telephone. He got the information in a very few minutes: Felicity was speaking from Wexham 32. Wexham, Longstaffe whispered, was a village about fifteen miles outside Highsea, on a by-road which meandered near the coast to Brighton.

"Do you know the address of the policeman there?" asked Dawlish.

"I'll get through to our man on a different line," said Longstaffe. "I'll tell him to go to the kiosk at once, and look after your wife."

"Many thanks," said Dawlish, gratefully.

He spoke to Felicity again.

"I was afraid you'd been cut off," she said. "Have you found anything out, Pat?" She still seemed nervous.

"Yes," Dawlish said, and told her to wait in the kiosk until the police arrived. He did not ask her what had happened, but told her he would be there in about half an hour. As soon as he had rung off, he wished that he had kept talking to her until the policeman arrived.

Longstaffe came back. "That's all right," he said; "our man was in. Now you want to go to Wexham, I suppose?"

"Yes, as quickly as I can."

"I don't think I'll come with you myself," said Longstaffe; "I'll find out if Harry May's finished on the cliff."

From then on events moved quickly. Dawlish preferred to drive his own car.

He was in no mood for talking. The only words spoken in the next twenty minutes were May's directions on the road. At last he said:

"Next turning right, and Wexham's about half a mile along the road."

Soon they pulled up outside a cottage. A blue sign reading *Police* shone outside.

Dawlish entered the small parlour and found Felicity sitting in an old arm-chair, with a cup of cocoa and some sandwiches in front of her.

She jumped up. "Hallo, darling!"

Dawlish gripped her hands. "Adventuring all alone, are you?"

"I *was* a fool!" admitted Felicity.

"What happened?" asked May, eagerly.

"It all seems so silly now it's over. I went in to see the Kinghams, and they were so overcome I didn't stay for many minutes. I walked back along the promenade, and was halfway along when I thought I was being followed. Like a fool, I decided to try and prove it," said Felicity. "Instead of hurrying back to the hotel, which I ought to have done, I took the side streets. And I proved that I was followed all right. In one of the darkest streets in Highsea—a man came out of the darkness, and I nearly jumped out of my skin."

"Go on," urged Dawlish.

"He was pleasant enough," said Felicity. "He said he was lost and wanted to find the Marine Hotel. So I said I was going there, and I felt rather glad to have company. Then, in the gateway of a house, I saw a car. It had no lights. The man took my arm, the next thing I knew I was in the car with a cloth over my head, and we were driving off. The man was in the back with me. I suppose we'd been travelling for ten minutes before he took the cloth away, told me to keep quiet and that no harm would come to me. Then—"

"Go on!" exclaimed May.

"The car stopped, and the man told me to get out. The moment while I was climbing down was one of the most frightening I've ever had. But the car moved off, leaving me in the road, without the faintest idea of where I was. I saw a light some way off, and walked towards it. The light came from the telephone-box, and

I called you immediately. There wasn't anyone watching me, it was a shadow. That—that's absolutely everything."

"But it's so pointless!" exclaimed May.

"It happened," Felicity said.

"I wonder if it is so pointless," murmured Dawlish, smiling at the stolid country policeman, who was standing by the door. "Not a bad opening move in a war of nerves, is it?"

"What on earth are you talking about?" demanded May.

"Wars of nerves," said Dawlish. "Supposing someone wants to scare me, or scare my wife?"

"Can you tell me why they should do anything like that?"

"Yes," said Dawlish. "They think I'm making a nuisance of myself."

"I wonder," said May, a little heavily. "Have you told us everything, Dawlish?"

"Yes," said Dawlish, mendaciously.

"I can't help feeling that you knew what was likely to happen when you came to Highsea," May declared. "This is not the beginning of the business for you, is it?"

Dawlish laughed. "Yes, most decidedly."

"*And* it's the end," declared Felicity.

Sitting next to Dawlish on the way back, she said nothing, although May was on edge on the back seat, hoping to catch anything that was said. He believed that Dawlish was keeping material facts away from the police. Dawlish, with only the story of Lancing's vendetta against Galloway on his conscience, wondered how easy it would be to dispel the suspicion.

They drew up outside the Marine Hotel a little after midnight.

"Can I drive you anywhere?" Dawlish asked May.

"No, I'm only a few minutes' walk from the station," May said. He added: "Dawlish, I hope you aren't putting anything across us. This is a murder case, you know."

"I know," said Dawlish. "And I also know you're barking up the wrong tree, old chap."

May grunted, and went off.

Dawlish and Felicity hurried upstairs in silence. In their room she looked tired out.

"I could sleep for a week! What happened when you followed White?"

Dawlish told her, and she listened with increasing anxiety while he went through that story again.

Only then did Dawlish begin to wonder whether she had told him everything.

She was too pale, too worried, for his liking. She had often undergone more trying adventures than tonight's, and had hardly turned a hair. Something had frightened her badly, and vividly he recalled her woebegone voice when she had spoken to him from Wexham. He finished his narrative.

"So that's what May meant when he said it was a murder case?"

"You mustn't sit there any longer," said Dawlish, "you look washed out. Let's get to bed. The world will be a brighter place in the morning."

She shivered. "Pat—"

"Hm-hm?"

"Can't we go home in the morning?"

"It won't be easy to leave at this stage," Dawlish said, taking her seriously. "Any special reason for wanting to go home?"

"Oh, no," said Felicity. "Only—I wish we hadn't come. I know it was my fault, I could kick myself for having suggested it."

She fell silent as she undressed.

Dawlish did not press her to talk; he suspected there was something else on her mind. Why wasn't she frank?

They had been in bed for twenty minutes.

"Pat."

"Hallo, my sweet." He pretended to sound sleepy.

"Tired?"

"I am rather."

"It doesn't matter, then," said Felicity.

Dawlish sat up. The light from the street lamps shone on the wall and the ceiling. He could see her hair spread out on the pillows.

"I'm wide awake now," he said. "What's troubling you?"

"That car-ride."

"You weren't hurt, were you?"

"No," said Felicity. "I wasn't hurt. I didn't tell the police everything, though."

"Didn't you?" asked Dawlish, quietly.

"The man said much more than I told you," said Felicity. "Darling, he scared the very wits out of me, but it sounds so absurd. I meant to sleep on it before I told you."

"But how did he scare you?"

"I wish I could explain *just* how he sounded," said Felicity. "He was a small man, Pat, with a cold voice. We were sitting in the darkness of the car, and the driver was going at high speed. Quite suddenly, he said, 'Supposing I opened the door and pushed you out, Mrs. Dawlish.' It went through me like a knife. I didn't answer. There was another pause, and then he added: 'I could do it quite easily. You would probably break your neck.' Then he stopped again. That was what made it so frightening, Pat. Those silences in between. I could almost feel myself hitting the road. The next time he said, 'I don't want to do it, but your husband is making a nuisance of himself, he mustn't continue doing so. The best way to make him realize it would be to push you out.' And then," added Felicity, "he opened the door."

Dawlish drew in a sharp breath. Felicity was snuggled close to his side, and he guessed that there were tears in her eyes. He felt her tighten her grip on his arm.

"Then he tapped on the driver's shoulder," said Felicity, "and the car stopped and they made me get out. That's all. You can understand how I felt, can't you?"

"I'll say I can!" exclaimed Dawlish.

"He didn't even tell me to tell you to leave Highsea," Felicity went on. "It was his coldness that worried me."

"I can see that, too," said Dawlish.

"*Can* we leave it now?" asked Felicity, and then added: "Of course, I know we can't. The man must have been speaking for Galloway. You haven't made a nuisance of yourself with anyone else, have you?"

"No, only Galloway," said Dawlish. "Hadn't we better sleep on it?"

"I am feeling sleepy now," admitted Felicity.

Soon she was asleep, but Dawlish lay awake, staring at the light on the ceiling. There was no real reason why he should not leave Highsea and let the police work the whole thing out.

Suddenly Dawlish had a mental picture of a man flinging himself in front of a train at Baker Street Station.

It was some time before he fell asleep.

Galloway was not asleep, although he was in bed. Abbott, still fully dressed, was sitting in an easy chair by his side. For some minutes Galloway had said nothing, but had stared bleakly towards his secretary, who had a pencil and note-book in his hands.

Galloway spoke. "I can't make up my mind, Abbott, whether I ought to let that cheque be paid or not, but I must be careful. Are you sure that his wife had no idea who was in the car with her?"

"I'm quite sure," said Abbott, "and I'm equally sure that I frightened her stiff." He sounded smug. "She really thought I was going to throw her out of the car!"

"Yes, you have your good points," Galloway said without enthusiasm. "The question is whether she will be able to persuade Dawlish to give up. On the whole, I think it will be better if I let the Kingham cheque go through. I might even make *him* an offer of a few thousand pounds, to help to offset his personal loss," added Galloway, more brightly. "In spite of what he says, that's what he really wants, I think. I don't believe in these people who pretend to want only to work for others. What do you think of that, Abbott?"

"It might work," admitted Abbott, cautiously.

"I'll let the cheque go through, and then see what Dawlish has to say tomorrow," decided Galloway, more brightly. "I think we had better stay here for a few days, Abbott. All right, you may go to bed."

Abbott jumped up. "Good night, sir."

"Good night," said Galloway, and switched off the light.

He was asleep half an hour later.

He did not hear the sound at the window, nor see the curtains billow as the window was opened wider.

A man climbed in, stepped softly to the floor, and stood watching Galloway as he slept. He made no sound. He moved towards the millionaire. He wore a dark handkerchief over the lower part of his face and a cloth cap pulled low over his eyes.

He took a small wash-leather bag from his pocket and extracted a sponge and a small bottle. A faint odour of chloroform filled the room. He poured a little on the sponge. Galloway slept with his mouth open, and breathed heavily.

The man put the pad over his mouth and nose.

Galloway jumped in his sleep, and woke up. He tried to cry out, but the pressure of the man's hand on his face was too firm. He tried to struggle, but could not get the chloroform pad away. After a few seconds his struggles ceased. His eyes closed and his body sagged. The man smiled beneath his scarf. Then he put the pad back in the bag, and turned to the wardrobe, where Galloway's clothes were hanging.

CHAPTER NINE

BRIGHT MORNING

"Well," asked Dawlish, "how do you feel this morning?"

"A hag," said Felicity.

"Apart from that?"

Felicity laughed. "You beast! I shan't really be happy until you've found the man in that car and treated him as he treated me."

They were sitting up in bed, and drinking tea.

"So we're not going to leave," said Dawlish.

"How can we?" asked Felicity. "I've been thinking it over. There are those people like the Kinghams and that man Milsom. Galloway is nervous. You might be able to do something for some of the others."

"What do you think of sending for Tim?"

"And Ted," suggested Felicity.

"Ted probably can't make it, but Tim would come like a shot. So would Freddie Armstrong."

"You might ring Tim, anyhow," said Felicity.

"I'll strike the old iron while it's hot! I always like waking Tim up."

Timothy Jeremy, who had worked with Dawlish in the

Intelligence Department, had first met him in the case when Felicity had been involved. Freddie Armstrong was a comparative newcomer to the small circle of Dawlish's close friends. Freddie had repeatedly voiced the pious hope that if Dawlish ever struck anything of the kind again, he should be included in the prospective corpses. For Freddie was a clown.

The ringing sound was in Dawlish's ears for a long time. At last, however, the sound stopped. There was a crashing noise. Immediately afterwards, a deep voice said:

"Who's that?"

"Santa Claus," said Dawlish.

"Eh?" ejaculated Tim.

"Some call him Father Christmas," declared Dawlish.

"Is that YOU?" cried Tim. "You oaf! You made me knock the lamp over. Damn it, I didn't get in until four o'clock. Great Scott! it's not half past eight! Call me later."

"But you've got such a busy morning," protested Dawlish.

"I haven't. I'm lunching with Freddie, and—"

"A very busy morning," insisted Dawlish.

"What are you driving at?"

"I want you to make one or two calls for me," said Dawlish. "We're down at Highsea—"

"What on earth you want to go to that dead-and-alive hole for I don't know," said Tim.

"There's something I want. Once upon a time there was a financier named Lancing, Giles Lancing, the great man of the Lancing Trust. He went bankrupt. He has a daughter, who lives alone in a flat in Kensington. I don't know what she looks like, Tim, but I would like to know something about her."

"What is this?" demanded Tim, much more soberly.

"Business," said Dawlish. "A bad business, too. You remember the *Hedshire Estates*?"

"A fool and his money," quoth Tim, and stopped.

"That's enough of that. I'm staying at the same hotel as Galloway. Someone tried to poison him. Someone else was pushed over the cliff."

"Do you know," said Tim, blandly, "I've often wanted to go to Highsea. Is Freddie in this?"

"If he feels like it."

"He will. We were only saying last night—"

"The name is Miss Lancing," said Dawlish, "and she goes out to work. You may have a job to find her. Ask Bill Trivett to lend a hand if you find it difficult. The Highsea Police have probably told him that I'm down here, so he shouldn't be surprised."

"It's coming to a pretty pass if I have to go to Scotland Yard about a little thing like that," said Tim. "We'll come down after lunch. Do you want us to bring the lady with us?"

"Not unless she feels like a day beside the seaside," said Dawlish. "All I want to know is what she thinks of Galloway."

Dawlish smiled as he rang off.

Felicity came in, flushed from a hot bath. "Have you spoken to Tim?"

"Yes. He's as lively as ever."

"That's fine," said Felicity. "Hurry with your bath, sweet, I'm famished."

Yes, thought Dawlish as they went downstairs to the dining-room, it was a bright morning. They sat at a window-table and were fussed over by the head waiter.

"Has Mr. Galloway come down yet?" asked Dawlish.

"I believe he is having breakfast in his room, sir."

"I see," said Dawlish. "Thanks."

"Are you going to make him telephone his London bank?" asked Felicity.

"As I've threatened to, I think I'd better," said Dawlish. "He may think that I'm getting cold feet if I don't. If he was behind last night's trick with you, my sweet, that would give him a lot of satisfaction."

Felicity went on to the verandah after breakfast.

Then she opened her newspaper and read the account of White's murder.

Meanwhile, Dawlish went upstairs to Galloway's suite. A different policeman was on duty in the passage. He looked at Dawlish warily.

Abbott opened the door.

"Good morning," said Dawlish, cheerfully. "Is Mr. Galloway up?"

"He is still resting, sir," said Abbott, "and I am afraid he will not be able to see you this morning, but—"

"Don't you think he might change his mind?" asked Dawlish.

Abbott looked anxious. "I hope you won't insist, sir. Mr. Galloway is feeling unwell. He has, however, given me instructions to telephone his bankers and to authorize the payment of the cheque, and he wishes me to assure you that he will honour his bond in *every* way. I do hope you will accept my assurance, sir."

Dawlish said: "The trouble is, can I? Ask Mr. Galloway to spare me two minutes."

"But—"

"Now, now," said Dawlish, warningly.

He was quite sure that Abbott was really on tenterhooks. He was equally sure that Galloway had left that message in the hope of persuading him to leave at once. Dawlish was extremely curious about the reason. It was not the reception he had expected, and suggested that something had happened to put Galloway into a more amenable frame of mind.

He heard Galloway's voice through the open door:

"No, Abbott, after all I have been through—"

'Hallo!' thought Dawlish, and stepped quickly to the door.

Galloway was sitting up on his pillows. His lips and nose were red, swollen and tender-looking.

Dawlish advanced towards the bed.

"Well, this is a sorry sight!" he declared, ironically. "By Jove, your lips look tender. And your nose." At close quarters he could see how sore they were. "They almost look as if they have been burnt, Galloway. Chloroform leaves a mess like that, doesn't it? Has Abbott been playing tricks in the night?"

Galloway sat up. "Abbott! If I thought—"

"But I was in my room, fast asleep," cried Abbott. "Of course I had nothing to do with it."

Galloway shot out his hand and gripped the man's wrist. Abbott winced. "I never thought of that." Galloway went on: "*Did* you do it, Abbott? It is remarkable how a man got in, with a policeman on duty outside all night." He glanced up at Dawlish, while retaining his grasp on Abbott's wrist. "I am indebted to you, Dawlish, for giving me the idea. I think I will look through your luggage, Abbott."

He twisted. Abbott gasped with pain, and staggered away.

The expression on Galloway's face was very much the same as it had been when he had attacked Miss Kingham. It passed in a flash. Galloway flung back the clothes, got out of bed and dragged his slippers nearer him.

"*Thank* you, Dawlish," he repeated. "If you will be good enough to keep an eye on Abbott for me, I will be grateful."

"A pleasure," murmured Dawlish, and wondered what had come over the man.

At times the man was clever; now he was behaving like a fool. Dawlish now knew that someone had broken into his room and chloroformed him, which suggested that Galloway had been robbed.

Abbott muttered: "Damn you, Dawlish, I didn't do it. You don't know what might happen now; he's—"

"Well, what is he?" demanded Dawlish. They could hear Galloway moving about in Abbott's room next door.

"Never mind," said Abbott.

The man was really on edge, desperately afraid of his employer. Dawlish was interested in the possibility of getting other information from him in this agitated frame of mind.

Abbott was staring at the open door.

"What time did you get back from Wexham?" Dawlish asked casually.

"Oh, before—" began Abbott, and then he realized what he was saying and what Dawlish was driving at. "I don't know what you're talking about!" he snapped. "Where's Wexham?"

Dawlish was smiling serenely. "Where you took my wife last night."

"Don't be a fool!"

"I don't like people who try to frighten my wife," murmured Dawlish, now quite sure that he was right. "Do you know that the police are looking for her assailant and that I am waiting to make a charge of assault?"

"You can't charge me," muttered Abbott.

"You'll see," said Dawlish.

Galloway returned.

"Well, did you find anything?" demanded Abbott, for once defiant.

"No, I did not. But you have been out this morning, Abbott. I am not at all sure that I can trust you." He stood there in royal blue pyjamas, his hair on end, his face still red and puffy, and he looked comical.

Dawlish asked gently, "What do the police think?"

Galloway turned on him. "I have not consulted the police,"

he said, "and I hope you won't tell them; the matter is quite personal, and—"

Dawlish laughed. "You are a fool, Galloway. The police are bound to find out sooner or later."

"How can they find out?" demanded Galloway.

"The chambermaid might talk about your appearance," Dawlish said. "Your face won't get better for two or three days, and if you shut yourself up in here for that time the police will want to know why; what harm is there in telling them that you were attacked again, and that your room was burgled?"

Galloway regarded him with narrowed eyes.

"Yes, I'm serious," Dawlish assured him. "What did happen last night? Was anything taken?"

Galloway snapped: "Yes, over a hundred pounds, my watch and several other pieces of jewellery. But you know my anxiety not to tell the police too much."

"Please yourself," said Dawlish. "I think I'm beginning to understand you."

"That's what *you* think," Galloway retorted, childishly.

Dawlish shrugged his shoulders. "I didn't come to give you advice," he said, "I came to hear you telephone your bank. It's a little after ten o'clock now, and Miss Kingham will be near the bank, I imagine."

He expected difficulty; he had none at all. Galloway lifted the receiver, and gave a London number.

"This is Galloway . . . I have sent a young lady to cash a cheque for a thousand pounds this morning. The number of the cheque is XK 224314. Honour it, please . . . Yes, all right, ring me back." He replaced the receiver. "The manager is going to ring me back, to make sure that someone is not speaking in my name," he said. "Does that satisfy you?"

"Reasonably," said Dawlish.

"What do you mean? I told you last night I won't stand for blackmail, and—"

"You also sent Abbott to take my wife for a ride last night," said Dawlish, "and I won't stand for that."

"I did no such thing!"

"I shall have no difficulty in proving it. What I haven't yet decided is whether to tell the police what I know. By the time they know everything they will be very curious about you."

"I tell you I know nothing about it." Galloway turned to Abbott. "Is Dawlish telling the truth?"

"Of course he's not."

"Abbott denies it," announced Galloway.

Dawlish laughed. "Galloway," he said, "I almost like you, in parts. All right, let's forget it. What did White come to see you about?"

"*White!*" exclaimed Abbott.

There was a hushed silence. Abbott was staring at Dawlish as if he could not believe his ears; even Galloway was taken aback. Dawlish needed no more telling that they had known White, and he imagined that they had reason to be afraid of the man.

Galloway said quietly, "What do you know about White?"

"Well, his Christian name is Jonathan, and—"

"He did not come to see me here. I give you my word."

Dawlish put his head on one side. "Well, he came to see me."

Just then the telephone call came through from London. Galloway dealt with it. Abbott, who had completely lost his head, turned and hurried out of the room.

Galloway turned from the telephone.

"What did White tell you?" he asked. "The usual story of looking after the interests of a number of people who had suffered in the *Hedshire Estates* failure, I suppose?"

"That and something more," said Dawlish.

"The man is a congenital liar," declared Galloway. "You are a fool if you believe him. He is not quite sane. He thinks that *Hedshire Estates* will recover their value, and he goes round buying up the worthless shares. That makes him appear a benevolent uncle in the eyes of the fools who lost their money. He must own nearly a quarter of *Hedshire Estates* stock, and he will never see a penny back for it." Galloway laughed. "He has some curious idea that I can make the land valuable. He is another of those who think that I am responsible for that failure, Dawlish. I am not."

"I see," said Dawlish.

"When did he come to see you?"

"Last night."

"Why didn't you tell me about this before?"

Dawlish murmured, "I didn't realize that I had to report to you, Galloway."

"Pay no attention to him. I have no doubt that he tried to buy the Kinghams' stock, and that of other people at Highsea who might have been on the stockholders list. I suppose he offered to buy *your* stock, Dawlish."

"No. He asked for my help," Dawlish said.

"To intercede with me, I suppose," guessed Galloway.

"You haven't read the newspapers this morning, have you?"

"I have no desire to see my name in the Press," Galloway said. "I have had too much unwanted publicity. I suppose they have given me a headline. I wish I had never allowed you to tell the police anything."

"*Allowed* me!" echoed Dawlish, weakly. Galloway did not seem to realize the absurdity of what he had said, and Dawlish went on gently, "There was something else in the newspapers."

"What?" demanded Galloway.

"Something about White—"

Galloway jumped up. "If that scoundrel has taken his story to the police, I'll have him in court for libel and slander. What did he say? Abbott! *Abbott!*" The secretary appeared in the doorway. "Get me the morning papers."

"Which papers, sir?" asked Abbott, humbly.

"All the papers, you fool! White's been talking. Hurry!" He waved Abbott away, then turned to Dawlish again. "I won't have these rumours that I am responsible for the *Hedshire Estates* failure."

"But White said nothing to the newspapers," Dawlish murmured.

"You just told me—"

"That there is something in the papers about him," Dawlish reminded him. "White was murdered last night."

Galloway stood quite still, staring at him.

"Do you mean that?"

"Of course I do."

There was a long silence, and then, to Dawlish's astonishment, Galloway began to laugh. "White is dead! You couldn't have pleased me more!"

He began to laugh again.

CHAPTER TEN

THE LOVELY LADY

Galloway's laughter still echoed in Dawlish's ears.

He went downstairs, and found Felicity. Felicity jumped up.

"Ready, Pat? How did you get on?"

"Pretty well," said Dawlish. "Yes, I think we'll have a walk." They strolled towards the embankment, which was crowded with cars and people.

"Well?" asked Felicity. "Has he paid it?"

"Yes."

"Triumph for Dawlish," said Felicity.

"I sometimes have the breaks," Dawlish said.

"There's still something on your mind, isn't there?"

"Much," admitted Dawlish. He told her that he was sure that Abbott was her abductor.

"Well, what else?" asked Felicity.

"Galloway's behaviour was the queerest mixture of the crafty, the cunning and the simple that I'm ever likely to come across," Dawlish told her. "I think I've discovered the truth about him. I mean, the truth about his manner. He's been so used to having his way that it's become a habit to expect it. He talked to me one moment as if I were a lackey waiting to obey orders, the next as if I were an old friend. I think he had such a shock during the night that he was hardly aware of what he was doing."

"What shock?"

Dawlish told her, and Felicity said enthusiastically:

"Splendid! He deserved all he got."

"Oh, yes," said Dawlish, "but don't you see the curious thing about it, darling? Someone did get into his room and chloroformed him. That someone could easily have murdered him. However, the opportunity was not taken. So there is one man who would like to see Galloway dead, another who wanted to rob him—and I do not believe that it was a common-or-garden burglar who made off with what loose cash there was in the room—and, to make the third angle, there is his crazy behaviour when he heard about White's murder. I can still hear him laughing."

Felicity looked at Dawlish soberly.

"Do you think he's sane?"

"There are moments when I begin to wonder," admitted Dawlish.

They reached the spot on the cliff where White had fallen over. Two policemen were on duty. A small crowd had gathered. They walked to the top of the cliffs, and were back in time for lunch.

Immediately after lunch Longstaffe came in. Dawlish thought him inwardly excited, although he started off quickly enough.

The car had not been found, but footprints and other evidence had been found, proving that there had been four men on the cliff at the time of the struggle. Inquiries were being made about White, and Longstaffe confirmed that in his pockets were some of the shares of *Hedshire Estates*. Then came the bombshell.

"And some strychnine, Dawlish! I've got two witnesses who saw him near the hotel yesterday."

Longstaffe was in no doubt that White had tried to poison

Galloway, and Dawlish thought the evidence was fairly convincing. White had seen him after the attempt probably to distract suspicion by making it seem that he needed Galloway alive.

In White's pocket, too, had been a blue pencil; that seemed to explain the marked newspaper. White was guilty on both counts.

Dawlish turned these things over in his mind, then asked how much White had paid for the shares.

"Two shillings each for one-pound shares," Longstaffe told him.

"Then his Highsea visit cost him a pretty penny," said Dawlish.

"Nearly four hundred pounds, altogether," Longstaffe said. "So he didn't think the shares were worthless. Have you learned anything more from Galloway?"

"I can tell you that Galloway was pleasantly surprised when he heard that White was dead," said Dawlish.

"Pleasantly!"

"Yes," said Dawlish, and explained more fully. He still withheld the whole story of Galloway's remarkable behaviour, however, and Felicity did not press him to explain why.

"What shall we do this afternoon?" she asked, when the policeman had gone.

"Listen to a band," suggested Dawlish.

They sauntered back to the hotel for tea a little before four o'clock. They went up to their room to wash, and Felicity went in first.

"What . . ." began Felicity.

Dawlish looked over her shoulder.

Sitting in an easy chair by the window was a woman—a lovely lady, smiling, beautiful. She stood up, gracefully. She was tall and smartly dressed. There was something vivacious about her.

"Good afternoon," greeted Felicity, a question in her voice.

"Good afternoon," said the lovely lady.

"And to what do we owe the pleasure of this visit?" asked Dawlish, heavily.

"Indirectly, to Mr. Galloway," she told him.

"How did you get in?" asked Felicity.

"The door was unlocked."

"Isn't that rather an old story?" asked Felicity tartly.

"Perhaps it is," said the lovely lady, who seemed amused by her reception, "but it's a true one."

Dawlish squeezed Felicity's arm, knowing that she felt annoyed and not wanting her to say anything which might shorten the interview. "Do sit down, Miss—"

"Lancing," said the visitor.

Felicity sent Dawlish a startled glance. Dawlish seemed to hear Galloway's voice, telling him that Giles Lancing's daughter had lived at his home for some time but now had a flat in Kensington. If this were the same girl, Tim Jeremy was trying to find her in London.

"Giles Lancing's daughter?" asked Dawlish.

"Yes," she said. "What do you know about my father?"

"Only the story that Galloway told me," said Dawlish.

"Galloway seldom tells the truth. Perhaps you've discovered that."

"There have been indications," admitted Dawlish. "How long have you been in Highsea, Miss Lancing?"

"I arrived an hour ago," she said. "When I saw the story in the newspapers this morning I left London as soon as I could. I hoped that it meant you—"

"Go on," urged Dawlish, encouragingly, and Felicity went and sat down, no longer looking annoyed.

"Are you trying to find out what Galloway is doing?" Miss Lancing asked.

"Up to a point," admitted Dawlish.

"I have been trying to find out for a year," she told him. "I didn't realize it was possible to dislike a man as much as I dislike Galloway. But then, I have particularly good reasons."

Dawlish murmured, "You are being a little mysterious, are not you?"

"I know I shouldn't have been waiting for you up here, Mrs. Dawlish, but I'd heard rumours that your husband was—well, a rather unusual person. I hoped that something unusual would attract his attention."

"He's unusual enough," admitted Felicity. "And you've succeeded."

The smile came back. "I'm so glad you're not angry! I'll be as concise as I can. My father and Galloway were once partners. They broke the partnership a few months before my father went bankrupt. I was at school. My mother always blamed Galloway, and so did my father's friends, but there was no proof—certainly nothing criminal. And there was enough money saved from the wreckage to enable us to live in reasonable comfort. I didn't give it much thought until a year ago," she said. "My father died after a long illness . . ."

Dawlish said, "He died?"

"Why, yes," she answered, startled.

"It doesn't matter," said Dawlish. "My interruption, I mean. Please go on."

"After his death I went through his papers. I found some old correspondence between Galloway and my father. Father accused Galloway of sharp practice; Galloway denied it and made counter-accusations. None of it made very pleasant reading," she went on, "but as my father broke the partnership afterwards I felt satisfied that the fault was Galloway's."

"That's easy to believe," said Dawlish.

She smiled. "Thank you. Perhaps I ought to explain that a few years earlier my father had gone to America. I lived at home with my mother, who died five years ago. I was rather lonely and quite young, and I felt very grateful when Galloway offered to give me a home. I was there for two years. By then I was growing up," she added. "He was much too friendly, and I decided to leave."

"Very sensible," murmured Dawlish.

"Then, about this time last year, my father came home," went on Miss Lancing. "He was a sick man. He lived only a few weeks. I had not known him since I was at school, and I had no great affection for him. It wasn't until afterwards, when I went through his papers, that I began to feel that he had received a very raw deal. The papers suggested that Galloway had been responsible for Father's failure. I consulted good friends of the family, who are of the same opinion. They all said the same thing, however: proving it would be a very difficult matter. I had no particular desire to prove it, but, as I say, I was satisfied that the blame lay on Galloway's shoulders. There didn't seem much point in raking up an old scandal."

"No," murmured Dawlish.

"So I was prepared to leave it, until Galloway came to see me. He wanted the old business records. He said that they belonged to him, as they concerned the days when he and Father had been partners. Of course, I refused to give them to him. He even threatened to take the matter into court. Galloway can never really understand it when anyone thwarts him."

Dawlish smiled reflectively at this confirmation of his own opinion.

"Well, that annoyed me, but I thought no more of it," Miss Lancing went on, "until my flat was burgled. Many of the papers were stolen. As it happened, I kept the correspondence between my father and Galloway in a separate case, and that wasn't touched. I felt pretty sure that Galloway was responsible for the burglary, and I began to wonder why he was so worried. It didn't take me long to understand why. Galloway was most anxious that no one else should see those papers. So I put them in a safe deposit, and when he came to offer to *buy* them, a fortnight later, I told him there was no deal, it opened my eyes to the real Galloway. I even thought of taking the correspondence to the police, but I thought that it might affect my father's reputation. Sentiment went against that, and I didn't particularly want to see Galloway in difficulties. I would have left it at that, but Galloway wouldn't stop worrying me for them. He didn't exactly threaten, but he was unpleasant. And then I met one or two people who had suffered in the *Hedshire Estates* affair. Galloway's name was freely mentioned. It was just about that time," she went on, "that I was nearly knocked down by a car when I was riding my bicycle along a side-street in Kensington. The car drove on, and I'm sure that Galloway's chauffeur was driving."

Dawlish straightened up. "Are you, by Jove?"

"What did you do?" asked Felicity.

"Nothing," answered the girl, "because there seemed very little I could do—the story sounded rather weak. I was always careful after that, though. Then I read in the papers about the attempt to poison Galloway, and that you were at this hotel, and I thought it might be a good idea to see you. So here I am."

"And very welcome," said Dawlish. "Have you had tea?"

"No, but—"

Dawlish leaned over and pressed the bell.

"We'll have it up here," he said. Then, "Your father came back to England last April, did he?"

"Yes."

"You're quite sure he was your father?"

The girl looked startled. "Yes, of course."

"Did you recognize him?"

"Perfectly well. I was seventeen when he left for America." She glanced at Felicity. "What on earth made him ask that?" she demanded.

Dawlish said, "Galloway told me that your father is carrying out a vendetta against him, and practically accused him of the attempt to poison him."

"What utter nonsense!"

"My opinion, too," said Dawlish. "It shouldn't be difficult to prove that he's lying. Have you still got those papers, Miss Lancing?"

She glanced down at a small suitcase on the floor.

"I brought them with me."

"Did you, by Jove!" exclaimed Dawlish. "When the girl's brought the tea in, we'll have a look at them."

And then, at a tap at the door, he added: "Come in. I'm ready for tea, aren't you?" He turned towards the door.

A man came in, holding a rifle.

CHAPTER ELEVEN

HOLD-UP

"Well, well," said Dawlish, blankly.

The man motioned for silence. He was short, thick-set, fair-haired, and wore a handkerchief over the lower half of his face.

"What do you want?" demanded Dawlish, heavily.

"Move over to that corner," the man said, gruffly. He motioned with the rifle. "Stand by the basin."

There was not much point in arguing. They stood in the corner watching the man, who immediately crossed the room, keeping a good distance from them.

"What do you want?" Dawlish demanded.

"Never you mind." The man glanced away from them, and his glance lit on Miss Lancing's case. He went to it. Facing them and keeping the rifle pointing towards them, the butt tucked under his arm, he bent down and picked the case up with his left hand.

"Now I see," murmured Dawlish. "A present for Galloway, I presume?"

"I don't know anyone named Galloway," said the man with the rifle, a shade too quickly. "Now don't you try any tricks, Dawlish, you stand still." He backed away from them, moving towards the door, still keeping them covered. "I don't want to hurt anyone," he added, "and—"

There was another tap at the door.

The man started violently, and nearly dropped the case. Dawlish took two steps forward, and was within two yards of him. The rifle moved sharply.

"Stay there! Tell them to go away."

Dawlish raised his voice. "What is it?"

"Your tea, sir."

"Tell her to put it outside," the man whispered urgently.

"Come in," called Dawlish.

The gunman swung round towards the door, trying to keep Dawlish covered at the same time. Dawlish shot out his hand and struck at the rifle. He knocked it flying. The man backed against the door as it opened. There was a crash, a gasp of dismay, and the noise of smashing crockery. Another cry, adding to the din, was followed by a gasp as Dawlish gripped his wrist.

Felicity was already moving towards the door.

"Keep her outside," whispered Dawlish.

Miss Lancing stood halfway between the door and Dawlish, while Felicity went out. She was full of apologies. She had fallen against the door, it was entirely her fault, the maid was not to worry. The maid, it proved, was tearful. Miss Lancing went out, and helped to clear up the mess, leaving Dawlish and the man alone in the room.

Dawlish kicked the suitcase under the bed, then pulled the man towards the window. He did not speak, and his captive seemed too scared. Not until Felicity and Miss Lancing returned, to report that the maid was on her way for another tray, did Dawlish pull down the handkerchief which covered the gunman's face.

He was a stranger to the Dawlishes.

"Do you know him, Miss Lancing?" asked Dawlish.

"No," she answered, promptly.

"That's odd," said Dawlish, "as he wanted your case."

"I didn't, I wanted *yours,*" snapped the gunman. "You needn't think I'm scared of you, Dawlish. You can't do anything to me." He was undoubtedly very frightened.

"We'll see," said Dawlish. "Who sent you?"

"None of your business!"

"Oh, don't be a fool," said Dawlish, and moved his right hand as if to strike the man on the face. The man backed away. Miss Lancing exclaimed. Dawlish moved his other hand and pulled the man's right coat-sleeve. He spun the fellow round, and a moment later stood with the coat in his hands.

He tossed the coat to the bed.

"Have a look through it," he said.

Felicity was already moving towards the coat. She took out a wallet and opened it, shaking the contents on the bed. The captive stared at her with growing concern. She picked up two letters, and said:

"They're both addressed to A. Martinson, at 2 A Gell Court, Notting Hill Gate."

"Now I wonder what 'A' stands for," murmured Dawlish foolishly. "Andrew, perhaps. Is there anything else there?" He watched Martinson closely all the time, and the man looked more scared than ever. There was a pause, while Felicity ran through the contents of the wallet.

"No, there's nothing much else," she said, "except two keys."

"I'll have a look at them in a moment," said Dawlish. "Well, Martinson, is there any good reason why we shouldn't hand you over to the police?"

"You wouldn't be such a fool!"

"So I'd be a fool, would I?" murmured Dawlish. "I wonder. "Darling, pick up his rifle—using a handkerchief; we don't want your prints on it—and keep him covered, will you?" When Felicity had done so, he went through the contents of the wallet. There were fifteen pounds in notes, stamps, membership cards of one or two clubs in London. The 'A' stood for Arnold.

"You know, you shouldn't carry your identity about with you," chided Dawlish, "it's most unprofessional. Turn round."

The man obeyed. Dawlish ran through his trousers pockets, found some silver, another bunch of keys, and a penknife with many blades. He examined the penknife closely.

"This isn't so amateurish," murmured Dawlish, "it looks like a professional cracksman's knife. What did you come for, Martinson?"

"I wanted your suitcase," Martinson repeated desperately; "I—I heard you'd cashed a big cheque this morning." Dawlish certainly did not believe him.

He picked up the keys and pressed them into a cake of soap, getting clear impressions. He made a note of the clubs of which Martinson was a member, and of several other things in the papers which had been found.

He gave the police-station number, and asked for Longstaffe.

Martinson swung round. "Dawlish! You won't—"

"I'm going to hand you over to the police," Dawlish said, and then Longstaffe came on the line. "I've a prisoner for you," Dawlish told him, and explained enough for Longstaffe to promise to come over himself.

Longstaffe arrived less than ten minutes after the telephone call. A sergeant was with him. The sergeant took Martinson away, but Longstaffe stayed, questioning Dawlish closely.

"And you hadn't cashed a cheque," Longstaffe said.

Dawlish laughed. "No, but here's a suggestion that might

explain his visit. Abbott and Galloway both knew that Miss Kingham had gone to London to cash that cheque, and Martinson might have overheard. He might even be in Galloway's employ. He would think himself on a good thing if he could come soon after Miss Kingham returned, and if he didn't know her he might get her mixed up with Miss Lancing."

"Yes, that's possible," agreed Longstaffe. "He wouldn't say anything more than you've told me?"

"Not a word," Dawlish said.

"And you haven't kept anything of his for yourself, I hope," said Longstaffe, with a chuckle. "I know your reputation."

"Everything that was in his pockets is on the bed," Dawlish assured him.

Longstaffe left a little after five o'clock.

As the door closed on Longstaffe, Muriel Lancing looked at Dawlish with a puzzled smile.

"Why didn't you tell him about the papers, Mr. Dawlish?" she asked.

"Because I have deep, secret thoughts about them and what we might be able to make of this business," Dawlish assured her. "Meanwhile, where are you staying tonight?"

"I haven't booked anywhere."

"They can probably find you a room here," said Dawlish. "Don't worry about the expense, we'll make Galloway pay for it."

Muriel allowed herself to be persuaded. Dawlish went downstairs to the reception-desk, and booked a single room.

A car drew up outside, and out of it stepped a man of rather less than medium height, and a round, comical face—Freddie Armstrong.

Dawlish moved a little to one side.

A taxi-driver brought in Freddie's luggage, and the porter took charge of it.

Freddie stood by the reception-desk, smiling at the girl who gave him the register to sign.

Dawlish approached him quietly and said, "Bo!"

Freddie started. A blot fell on the register.

"Confound your eyes, you made me jump. Well, well, Highsea agrees with you—look at your sunburn!" He patted Dawlish's shoulder. "I'll look after you from now on."

They were at last in the lift, on their own.

"Well, what's doing?" he demanded, in a different tone of voice. "Much, I hope. Tim's still chasing the girl Lancing. She left her office this morning, without telling anyone where she was going. The beggar sent me on in front of him, hoping to cover himself in glory by discovering her corpse or something. Do you think anything might have happened to her?"

"It's possible," admitted Dawlish, as they got out of the lift.

"How's the Galloway bird?"

Dawlish laughed. "I'll tell you all about it soon," he said. "Meanwhile, behave yourself, I'm going to introduce you to a really beautiful girl."

Dawlish opened the door of the bedroom.

On the bed, lashed back to back, were Felicity and Muriel.

Muriel was looking towards Dawlish. Her fine eyes were wide open, but there was a handkerchief tied about her mouth, so that she could not utter a sound. Felicity was also gagged.

Dawlish bent down and looked under the bed. The suitcase was not there. He glanced quickly about the room, as Freddie took out a penknife. He made sure that the case was not in the room, and swung round towards the door.

"Look after them," he said, and hurried out.

He ran along the passage, passing a startled resident, and then down the stairs, too impatient to wait for the lift. He reached the first floor. A policeman was on duty.

"Has anyone come out or gone in lately?" he demanded.

The policeman said, "Mr. Abbott just went in, sir."

"Carrying a case?"

"As a matter of fact, he was—" began the policeman.

Dawlish said, "Thanks." He turned and tried to open the door, but it was locked. He swung round again, took the first passage on the right and hurried to the fire escape which led to Galloway's rooms.

The back door opened without any trouble.

He stood for a moment, listening. There were voices in one of the other rooms.

"Hurry," Galloway was saying, "get that case out of the room; we mustn't—"

Dawlish flung the door open.

"Why, hallo," he said, "how nice to see you both again!"

They were standing by the table in Galloway's room. It was piled with folded papers. The empty suitcase lay on the floor.

Abbott stood at one end of the table, Galloway the other. A wood fire was burning in the grate near them.

Galloway gasped, "D-D-Dawlish!"

"Isn't it odd how I appear at inconvenient times?" murmured Dawlish. "Last night you tried to scare the life out of my wife and this afternoon you've manhandled her. I warned you that I didn't approve of that kind of behaviour."

He moved quickly enough to startle Galloway, yanked him forward, and put him over his knee. Abbott stared, petrified. Dawlish delivered half a dozen hearty spanks to Galloway's posterior and then pushed the man away from him. Galloway staggered to a chair, and leaned against it.

Dawlish turned to Abbott. "Pack the case," he said.

Abbott said, "I—"

"Pack it!" snapped Dawlish, and made as if to move towards

the man. Abbott did not hesitate any longer, but began to obey. Dawlish watched him, while keeping an eye on Galloway, who seemed to be recovering from the shock.

There was a tap at the outer door, and then the bell rang.

"Ask who it is," ordered Dawlish.

Galloway walked unsteadily towards the door, hesitated, and then said in an unexpectedly firm voice:

"Who is it?"

"Constable Evans, sir. Is everything all right in there?"

"Yes, of course," said Galloway, crossly. "Please don't worry me." He turned round, face expressionless.

"Now, Dawlish," Galloway said, mildly, "there are limits to what I will endure from you. I insist—"

"You aren't in a position to insist," said Dawlish. "Abbott watched your first messenger carted off to the police-station, and then tried for the case himself. He nearly got away with it. Martinson is with the police now. I don't think he'll betray you, but I certainly shall if I have any more trouble with you. Hurry up, Abbott."

Abbott said, "I-I can't get them all in."

"They were in before, weren't they?"

"Yes, but—"

"Oh!" cried Galloway, in a strangled voice. "Oh!" He staggered, and for a moment Dawlish thought that he had been taken ill.

For a second, however, he glanced at Abbott; there was a wealth of cunning in his eyes.

Abbott grabbed the papers and rushed with them to the grate.

Dawlish went after him, but Galloway tried to stop him. He brushed the millionaire aside, then pushed Abbott out of the way. Some of the papers had caught at the edges, but they were all tightly folded and would not burn easily. He snatched them out of the flames, scorching his fingers.

He turned and faced the others.

"You do want them badly," he observed. "I ought to find them interesting reading."

Neither of the others spoke.

"Worried about something?" asked Dawlish. "I suppose Muriel Lancing's arrival startled you, and made you act so foolishly. The police are most interested in you, and if they learned about the visit to my room they might take you away and put you in prison. If you play this game any more, I shall get really rough. I don't know what is behind it, but I do know that you are in a very awkward position."

Galloway said: "By withholding information from the police, Dawlish, you have weakened your position. Now, be reasonable. I can understand your annoyance. I deplore the fact that Abbott's visit was necessary. And if it is proved that Abbott used unnecessary violence, then I shall be most severe with him. He assured me that he did not. It is useless for me to pretend that I did *not* send for this case. It is Miss Lancing's case; you have hardly any right to the contents. I have *every* right. Those papers are confidential papers which her father wrongfully withheld from me, and I could undoubtedly prove my right to them. Whereas by your violence here, Dawlish, you would find yourself in great difficulties if the matter were taken into court. Let us be reasonable. Tell me what you want from that case, and I will do my best to satisfy your requirements."

Dawlish stared at him owlishly.

"What papers do you want?"

"All of them," said Dawlish.

"Oh, come! If there are any of private character, which rightly belong to Miss Lancing, I will see that she has them." When Dawlish did not answer, he went on in a stronger voice: "I was hoping to have a talk with you, Dawlish, I have a proposition to put to you."

"Oh!" said Dawlish, blankly.

"And I feel sure that you will find it reasonable," Galloway went on. "I know that your chief interest is to regain the money which you lost. I sympathize with you—I am prepared to pay you a sum equivalent to one half of what you have lost." When Dawlish made no answer he went on a trifle hurriedly: "I had fully made up my mind to do that before you came in. In the new circumstances, I can be a little more—er—benevolent. I will reimburse you eight thousand pounds. As a consideration, you will allow me to take what papers I require. To prove that I intend to make no use of them, I will burn them in front of your eyes. Well, Dawlish?"

CHAPTER TWELVE

COUNCIL OF WAR

Dawlish turned to Abbott, and told him to make a parcel of the papers.

"And put the clothes in the case," said Dawlish.

Galloway moved forward. "You have not yet replied to my offer, Dawlish. Perhaps you would feel *completely* happy if I were to—Yes, I will!" He clapped his hands together. "Indeed I will, Dawlish—I will make you a payment of eleven thousand pounds! That is, complete restitution. I will write out the cheque now."

"I shouldn't bother," said Dawlish.

"You do not *refuse*!"

"But I do," said Dawlish.

"Dawlish! You cannot be so foolish as to reject my offer."

"Rejected," said Dawlish. He looked at Abbott, who had tied the parcel up. "Close the case," he said, and went across the room and picked up both case and parcel. "I'll see you later," he promised.

"Dawlish!" Galloway stood in the doorway. "You will not leave this room."

"If you make any more trouble, I shall go straight to the police with the papers and with this story," said Dawlish, sharply.

"*You will not leave this room!*"

Dawlish walked towards him. Galloway looked an insignificant little man. He waited until the last moment, and then put his hand to his pocket.

Dawlish dropped both case and parcel and grabbed him. Dawlish swung him round and put his hand into the pocket. He drew out a small automatic.

He held it on the palm of his hand, and said wonderingly:

"My wife did wonder whether you were sane, and I'm wondering with her now." He was genuinely astonished at the move.

Galloway did not speak.

Dawlish put the automatic in his pocket and picked up the parcel and the case.

"Very many thanks indeed," he said. "Good-bye."

The door closed on him.

"How—how did you get in *there?*" demanded the policeman.

Dawlish laughed. "I wanted to surprise my friends, and used the emergency door. I'll have a word with the Superintendent about it a little later."

"I see, sir." The man spoke doubtfully.

When he returned to his own room, the girls were sitting in easy chairs. Freddie Armstrong was standing between them.

"Pat, my boy," chided Freddie, "you scared us; we were afraid something had happened to you. What have you got there?"

"A present from Galloway," said Dawlish, brightly.

"Isn't that Muriel's case?" demanded Felicity.

"Yes. The papers are in the parcel, scorched but not seriously damaged, I think. Your assailant was Abbott, the secretary, and they were examining the case as I went in. They had quite a shock."

He told them what had happened as he washed his hands. There were two blisters, and Felicity dabbed aquaflavine on them.

Muriel had not uttered a word since his return. When he had finished, Freddie said in a deep voice:

"I've heard that you do things like this, but I've never believed it before. Galloway must be mad."

"He certainly isn't normal," said Dawlish.

"But mustn't you tell the police?" asked Muriel, looking bewilderedly at Felicity. "I should have gone straight to the police after that. He must, mustn't he?"

Felicity raised her eyebrows. "Well, he should," she agreed. "Whether he will is a different matter."

"What on earth do we want to go to the police for?" demanded Freddie. "I'm surprised at you. This is our show."

"It might become our show," Dawlish admitted. "When's Tim coming?"

"He should be here any moment," Freddie said. "We've just had a telephone call from him. He caught the next train after mine. Why the sudden interest in Tim? He's got nothing to report."

"I'd like to have his opinion on this," Dawlish said, as he sat on the bed and leaned his head against the wall. "On the whole, I think a Council of War is necessary. The question is whether we can safely keep this latest incident from the police, and if we do, can we get any money back for the *Hedshire Estates* victims?"

Timothy Jeremy arrived ten minutes afterwards. He was a tall, lean man, good-looking, although his cheeks were too thin, and with enormous clear brown eyes.

That evening he came fresh from the journey, after belatedly discovering from a friend in Muriel's office that she had gone to Highsea, and listened attentively to the story, which Dawlish told the others from beginning to end.

Dawlish finished mildly: "So what we have to consider, I think, is whether we have Galloway in a weak enough position to work on him and make him disgorge his ill-gained profits out of the *Estates* deal."

Muriel spoke quickly. "Surely it's asking for trouble to keep all this from the police!"

Tim laughed. "Pat's always asking for trouble, and usually gets it. The question is less whether it's inviting more, but which will bring him the less. I'm not getting excited."

"Do you ever?" demanded Freddie.

Tim ignored him. "What does it boil down to? You haven't told the police the story Galloway told you. Well, hearsay isn't evidence. The worst they could do would be to reprimand you sharply. You told them the truth about White. You didn't tell them about the chloroform attack on Galloway. I suppose that was hearsay, too. It was pretty conclusive, but there's no reason why you should report a burglary if the man who was burgled wants it kept to himself. They *might* add the two things up to withholding material evidence, but I don't think it would work. What do you think, Pat?"

"I doubt if they could do anything, except make themselves unpleasant," said Dawlish. "Longstaffe has a feeling that I've got a powerful reason for being here, of course, and May is worried. They'll watch me in the hope that I do something silly. But on the whole they're well disposed."

"That's what I can't understand," admitted Muriel. "I would be scared out of my wits if I kept anything back from them in this way."

"There have been times when the police have asked Pat to

lend a hand," Tim reminded her. "That's an angle we might think about, Pat. Have a word with Trivett, he might suggest to Longstaffe and Company that it would be a good idea to let you have your head."

Dawlish said promptly: "No, it won't do. We've got to be quite independent of the police."

"That's true," admitted Tim, thoughtfully. "Well, what's next? This afternoon's bother, I suppose. You gave them Martinson. They haven't any reason to suspect that there was a second burglary. All they can know is that you made an unorthodox entry into Galloway's flat and came out with a parcel and a case. Provided Galloway doesn't lodge a complaint—"

"He won't," Dawlish said confidently.

"Then you've nothing to worry about." Tim smiled. "You made sure that Martinson wasn't going to admit that he was after Muriel's suitcase before you turned him over. A useful point."

"Thanks," said Dawlish, dryly.

"On the whole, I think we'll be safe enough to go on, provided we keep a watchful eye on the police," Tim declared. "What can go wrong? Only Galloway could make trouble, and his position is so weak that he isn't likely to, as you say. And he might be in an even weaker position when you know what's in those papers which Muriel brought along. The next item, then, is, will he cough up? When you say you think you might get him to reimburse the people who suffered in *Hedshire Estates,* do you mean 'all'?"

"Yes," said Dawlish.

Tim whistled. "A quarter of a million, wasn't it?"

"About that," admitted Dawlish. "But he's got the money. We could work this way, I think: get something on account, distribute it among the shareholders anonymously, try again, make a second distribution, and so on."

Tim said owlishly, "Of course, it is pretty nearly blackmail."

"A nice point," admitted Dawlish. "I half wish I'd accepted the eleven thousand, it would have been a beginning. Still, he'll make that offer again. I don't think he'll stay in Highsea much longer."

Muriel protested. "If the police do find out what you're doing?"

Dawlish smiled. "I don't think we need worry too much about being jailed," he said. "Galloway isn't going to give any one of us any money. He's going to put it into a pool, and the pool will distribute it. We can get some reputable and high-souled person to do the distributing. We might even get a firm of solicitors to handle it. As far as they are concerned, Galloway will send them a cheque every so often, with instructions to share it out among the holders of *Hedshire Estates* stock. All we do is frighten Galloway into parting with the money. We don't touch the money. To keep ourselves really safe, my name goes off the list of shareholders."

"That's hardly fair," Muriel protested.

"There isn't any choice," said Dawlish, "but there's one thing we have forgotten."

"What's that?"

"That White didn't go round buying *Hedshire Estates* out of the goodness of his heart," said Dawlish. "He paid two shillings a share, and you can be sure that he expected to make a profit. His story wasn't the whole truth, or he would have told me what he intended to do. And we know that White wanted Galloway dead."

"Question, what made White think there would be money in it?" observed Tim.

"Yes. That's a line we ought to follow," Dawlish said. "White will have friends." He took out his note-book and went on: "He lived at 17 Hollway Mansions, Chiswick. That's a job for one of you. He might have been married, or have had a housekeeper, or—"

"Do you mean to say that you've dragged us down here only to send us back to London?" demanded Freddie.

Tim laughed. "It's what you must learn to expect."

"*Are* you going to leave the next approach to Galloway to one of the others?" Muriel asked.

"I think so," said Dawlish.

"Well, then," suggested Muriel, "oughtn't you to go to London and leave Mr. Armstrong and Mr. Jeremy down here?"

Freddie went gravely to her and shook her hand.

"You are a woman after my own heart," he declared.

Dawlish laughed.

"Sorry, Freddie, I must stay to see which way Galloway jumps, and I don't think the police would take it kindly if I were to slide off."

"Oh!" said Freddie. "Pity. That in no way lessens my high regard for you," he added, and squeezed Muriel's hand. "I suppose you wouldn't like to come to London with me?"

"Need any of us go?" asked Tim, gently. "What's the matter with putting Ted on to this London angle, Pat?" A reminiscent smile hovered about his face. "Poor Ted! He's doing his best to look like a harassed parent. Joan's in the nursing-home, the offspring is expected any day, so he can't leave London, but he'd be pathetically grateful for something to do. He came with me this morning, and moaned and groaned because he couldn't come."

"I don't see why not," said Dawlish. "I'll ring him."

A mighty voice cried, "*Hallo!*" when he was put through to Ted Beresford's London flat, and when Dawlish announced himself, the voice trailed off. "Oh, it's you, is it," said Ted. "I thought it was from the nursing-home."

"How are things?" asked Dawlish, sympathetically.

"Life's awful," declared Ted. "The suspense is terrible." He chuckled. "The doctor tells me nothing is likely to happen for twenty-four hours. You *would* select this time to find a job out of London."

"As a matter of fact . . ." began Dawlish, and talked at some length. When he finished, Ted Beresford promised to have a full report on the other occupants of 17 Hollway Mansions and the life story of Jonathan White ready within twenty-four hours.

"Who is this Ted?" asked Muriel.

"An odd customer," said Freddie. "Lifelong friend of Pat's. As a matter of fact," he added, on a more serious note, "he was mixed up in a spot of Pat's special and lost a leg a couple of years ago."

Felicity said: "What are we going to do now, Pat?"

"Watch and wait," said Dawlish. "We might do a spot of preparatory work. We need a solicitor who can be relied on to see us through. We'll have to dig one up from somewhere."

"Do you seriously think that you'll be able to do this?" demanded Muriel.

"We can but try," said Dawlish, "and the papers you've brought us should be a help. Those papers were worth eleven thousand pounds to him, and they may well be worth more. Let's take some each, and go through them."

They set to work.

The scrutiny took nearly an hour. Dawlish was sitting at the dressing-table, his pipe between his lips, his expression set and wooden.

As he looked through the old papers, a picture built itself up in Dawlish's mind. It was not unlike the picture of misery and disaster which had followed the collapse of *Hedshire Estates.* There was the same trail of broken homes and hopeless men and women. He did not think that Giles Lancing came out of the deal too well, but Galloway's part in the earlier affair was glaringly obvious, and there was no reasonable doubt that he had been the direct cause of Lancing's failure. Dawlish doubted whether there had been anything illegal in any of the transaction. Two partners had fallen out, and Galloway had proved the stronger, and had also proved relentless in his determination to take revenge on Lancing.

There was every reason why Galloway should be anxious to destroy those papers.

He finished. The others were watching him. Dawlish was trying to create another picture with the pieces of the present puzzle which he had in his mind. First, White's attempt to murder Galloway, followed eventually by the chloroform attack, which, presumably, had been meant only to frighten Galloway. Then the murder of White, and Galloway's glee when he had heard of it. There was proof that Galloway had reason to be afraid of White, and surely linked up with White's purchase of the supposedly worthless shares. There, thought Dawlish, was the crux of the whole problem: why had White believed that *Hedshire Estates* would become valuable again?

There seemed only one likely answer.

Galloway, having made a fortune out of one handling of the affair, might have some scheme in mind to revive the value of the land which had been purchased. But if that were so, *he* would be buying the shares, or getting hold of them as best he could. It would not be done openly. If there were sudden large purchases on the Stock Exchange, the price would go up. White had behaved cautiously. Was Galloway also picking up what shares he could at a low rate?

In the middle of his thoughts there was a tap at the door. Felicity called, "Come in," and Galloway appeared on the threshold.

CHAPTER THIRTEEN

GALLOWAY IS HUMBLE

Dawlish was already standing in front of Galloway, who looked apprehensive and could not see into the room.

"What do you want?" Dawlish demanded, harshly.

"My dear sir, I come on a peaceful errand. I think that I can explain most of the misunderstanding."

"Oh, do you," growled Dawlish.

He had no objection to hearing what Galloway had to say, but he did not want the man to know that Muriel and the men were in the room.

"Are we in the way?" Tim called.

"Oh, I *do* beg your pardon," teetered Galloway. "You have guests. Can you spare me a few minutes when you are free?"

Dawlish said: "Yes. Come again in a quarter of an hour."

"You are so kind," murmured Galloway. He pranced off down the passage.

Dawlish closed the door.

Muriel was looking at him open-mouthed.

"How on earth did you manage that?" she demanded. "I've never known him so humble in my life!"

Dawlish smiled. "He's a very worried man, my dear."

"I take it you didn't want him to see her," said Tim, "and she dutifully faced the wall, but he knows she's here, doesn't he? It's a bit late in the day."

"Yes," said Dawlish, "but he doesn't know you and Freddie yet, and he'd probably be most interested to know how friendly Muriel is. Keep away from Muriel—"

"No, confound it—" Freddie began to protest.

"Needs must," said Dawlish, "and you'd better not be too obviously connected with me. Sorry to keep Freddie away from you," Dawlish added to Muriel.

"Oh, I don't mind that," said Muriel, making Freddie wince, "but I do want to hear what he says."

"We'll have to leave it to Pat," Tim said.

Freddie fingered his upper lip. "Need we?" he demanded. "Pat wouldn't keep secrets from us. There's an empty room with a communicating door next to mine—Room Thirty-two. If the interview is in there, we can keep the door open and hear all that takes place. I would like to hear Galloway eating humble pie. Any objections, Pat?"

"Wouldn't it look odd if Pat sees Galloway in another room?" asked Muriel.

Dawlish said thoughtfully: "Yes, but I don't think it would matter. The more we mystify the gentleman the easier meat he's going to be later on. You win, Freddie. What are your room numbers?"

"Thirty and Thirty-one."

"Yes, you use Thirty-one," suggested Dawlish; "I'll bring Galloway along to Thirty-two. Have the door just ajar. I'll make him stand with his back to it, and he'll notice nothing. Are you going with them or coming with me?" he asked Felicity.

"I'll come with you," said Felicity.

Exactly a quarter of an hour after they had left, Galloway returned and tapped timidly on the door. Dawlish made him jump when he gripped his arm.

"We're going down to the next floor." Galloway followed him meekly, with Felicity bringing up the rear.

They reached Room Thirty-two. Dawlish unlocked the door and let Felicity go in first. She stood by the communicating door, so that Galloway was not likely to notice that it was open. Dawlish closed and locked the door and dropped the key into his pocket.

"Sit down," said Dawlish.

Galloway obeyed.

"I do apologize for my earlier intrusion," he said. "One question, Dawlish. You are not trying to keep me away from Muriel Lancing, are you?"

"You can guess," Dawlish said, heavily.

"You are not being very helpful," protested Galloway.

"I do not intend to be helpful to you, Galloway. I dislike you intensely. I have not forgiven you for trying to scare the wits out of my wife. Taken by and large," went on Dawlish, shifting his position slightly, "I think you are a liar, a knave, a scoundrel, a bully, a fool, a braggart and a worthless piece of humanity."

"D-D-Dawlish!" Galloway's voice squeaked. "I am hurt, I am aghast to think that any man could have such a poor impression of *me*. I—I cannot tell you how distressed I am. I hold you in very high esteem, Dawlish. And I came to make that clear, to make it apparent for you to see." He covered his eyes with his hand, and appealed, "How—how can I make you revise your opinion of me, Dawlish?"

"You mean how can you stop me from going to the police," said Dawlish, roughly.

"No, no, you wrong me," protested Galloway. "I have simply

tried to regain what is my own; it is true that I tried to frighten you by showing an automatic, you perhaps forget one thing—there was no witness except Abbott, who is a faithful servant. You have a poor opinion of me, I have a high opinion of you. Nothing you ever do will alter my opinion, but I am still hopeful of altering yours. That is why I have come."

"Go on," said Dawlish.

"I made you a substantial offer, enough to recoup you for your losses in *Hedshire Estates.* You scornfully rejected it. I appreciate your motives. I have not had the pleasure before of meeting men as high-minded as yourself. At last, I said to myself, I have encountered a man who puts the interests of other people high above his own. And so, Dawlish, I have come"—he leaned forward and raised his hand to emphasize his words—"*I have come to throw myself upon your mercy.*"

"Oh," said Dawlish, startled out of his pose.

"I have indeed," said Galloway. "Dawlish, you know the truth. My life is in danger. I am frightened. I have no faith in the police, but I have a great faith in *you.* So I come with a proposition. Put your services at my disposal, Dawlish. Try to find the man who is attempting to murder me. And for reward—money for the unfortunate victims of the *Hedshire Estates* failure. For your services I will give *twenty-five thousand pounds,*" he repeated with bated breath, "for you to distribute among those victims. Dawlish, *can* I do more?"

Dawlish remained silent for a moment. Then:

"But don't you know the name of the man? Didn't you tell me that it is Lancing?"

Galloway raised his hands. "I did tell you that, yes. The truth is that a *partner* of Giles Lancing is probably concerned. Lancing himself died on his return to England, about a year ago. You see, I am being completely frank."

"I see," said Dawlish; he had doubtless changed his story because Muriel had turned up.

"I do not even demand that you succeed in your mission before receiving the reward," Galloway said. "I am a judge of men. I know that you will do everything in your power. I will make that payment *now.*"

"I see," said Dawlish.

"Does not the suggestion appear to you to be fair, generous, and proof of my goodwill?" asked Galloway, eagerly.

"It could be," said Dawlish, slowly. "All right, I'll buy it."

"You *will!*" Galloway jumped from his chair and rushed forward, seizing Dawlish's hands. "I cannot tell you how delighted I am!"

He drew back, and took a cheque-book from his pocket.

"But we must have an agreement about this," Dawlish said. "My word—"

"Is more than sufficient for me!" cried Galloway.

"But not for me," said Dawlish, racking his brains for the name of a solicitor on whom he could rely in such an emergency. "Make out the cheque to Graham, Pearce and Graham, will you?"

"But surely you will be the administrator . . ." began Galloway.

"No, Graham, Pearce and Graham will look after it," said Dawlish. "They're quite reliable. And they'll want a letter from you, instructing them what to do. Something like this: 'I am enclosing a cheque for £25,000, for distribution among shareholders in the *Hedshire Estates,* at the discretion of your good selves, Mr. Patrick Dawlish and—and Superintendent William Trivett, of New Scotland Yard.'" Galloway was looking nonplussed and a trifle uneasy; he bent over the dressing-table with his pen in his hand. "'This contribution is made in consideration of services about to be rendered to me by Mr. Patrick

Dawlish.' Yes," went on Dawlish, with a gentle smile, "that about covers it."

"I'll get some notepaper," Felicity said, quickly.

"There's some in that writing-table," Dawlish said, pointing; "if you'll write it, to save Mr. Galloway the trouble . . ."

"It is a great deal of money," said Galloway, "but for my peace of mind it is well worth while." He signed the cheque with a flourish. Felicity was writing furiously, and he turned towards her. "My life is very precious to me, Mrs. Dawlish," he said, gently.

"And it's very precious to me," said Dawlish, feelingly.

Among the Dawlishes and their friends, not least Muriel Lancing, there was a curious tension. It was almost as if Galloway had overheard their plans and had determined to get them off to a good start. Now and again Freddie demanded another glance at the cheque, and each time threw up his hands in bewilderment.

They had discussed the affair. They had discovered no snag. The most reasonable suggestion was from Muriel. Galloway, being incredibly rich, could well afford twenty-five thousand pounds for his own peace of mind. It was most likely that he wanted only to stop Dawlish from pursuing him.

Longstaffe came in and put an end to their idle deliberations. He had little to say, and no fresh information. When he had gone they decided to go to bed. They decided, also, that the men should take it in turns to watch Galloway's rooms. True, there was a policeman on duty still, but, as Dawlish said, they must carry out their share of the bargain.

Nothing happened that night.

Next morning Dawlish telephoned Arthur Graham, the junior partner in the firm of Graham, Pearce and Graham, who agreed to act with alacrity. A little after two o'clock Graham telephoned Dawlish. Galloway had sent a special messenger, telling him what to expect and charging him to take every precaution to make the distribution fair to all concerned.

The following morning the cheque reached Graham, who made a special clearance on it and rang through to tell Dawlish that it had been cleared and the money was now in a separate account, awaiting his instructions. That morning, too, Superintendent Trivett telephoned from London and wanted to know what the devil Dawlish was playing at.

"I don't know what you're up to, Pat, but don't take too many chances. Galloway is powerful, you know. Blackmail's an ugly word."

Dawlish laughed.

"The local people are admirable men, but they aren't making much progress in the White case, are they?"

"No," said Trivett. "We're sending someone down to lend them a hand—Sam Davy. With you in the background, I wish I could come myself. Pat, I'm serious—be careful."

"You need have no fear," said Dawlish, and after a few moments' conversation he rang off.

Felicity was in the room with him. Muriel was out in the town. Tim and Freddie were in their rooms.

Galloway did not come near them.

Ted Beresford had been able to learn little about White, who had lived in a service flat, on his own. In his office, which was near the flat, two harassed young girls worked, dealing with correspondence and with the police. Ted, by then, was distracted. The new arrival was taking an unconscionable time coming.

Longstaffe and Davy, from Scotland Yard, came in to see Dawlish, and in the course of conversation let Dawlish know that in Jonathan White's office there had been a duplicate list of the names and addresses of *Hedshire Estates* victims, but no record at all that White had bought any other *Estates* shares. There was no further reason, Longstaffe said, for Dawlish to stay in Highsea if he wanted to leave.

Galloway spent most of his time sunning himself. He told Dawlish that he felt twenty times more secure, and that he would tell Dawlish the whole story and set him to work when he had finished his holiday. He intended to stay in Highsea for another week.

On the Saturday, when the hotel bill was due, Dawlish discovered a receipted bill in his room. Muriel came hurrying in from hers, a little put out. Pat should not have paid her account . . .

"But I didn't," protested Dawlish.

"Well, it's been paid."

"So has ours," said Dawlish, raising an eyebrow. "Mr. Galloway is still being generous, I fancy."

"It just doesn't make sense," said Muriel. "But I must get back to work. You'll have to stay as long as Galloway does, I suppose?"

"Yes," said Dawlish.

"Do you think everything is over?" asked Muriel. "Everything is so quiet that—"

"Suspiciously quiet," Dawlish said, cheerfully. "But we'll keep you informed. Freddie is going back tomorrow, too; he'll probably keep a seat on the train for you."

It crossed Dawlish's mind that Muriel had lost most of her natural gaiety.

It was in that atmosphere of incredulous suspension that they went to bed that night, and during the night Galloway disappeared.

CHAPTER FOURTEEN

BIRD FLOWN

Longstaffe had taken away the police guard from outside Galloway's suite the night before. Dawlish had continued it, and he and Tim had watched in shifts until four o'clock, leaving Freddie to take the last shift, under protest.

At half past four Freddie decided that he wanted a drink.

He was away from the door for only seven minutes. In that seven minutes, it seemed, the damage was done.

Dawlish did not even know there was any cause for alarm, and was shaving alone in the room. It was then a little after eight o'clock. The next moment there was a thunderous banging on the door, which burst open; Abbott rushed into the room.

"Why, hallo," said Dawlish. "What's this?"

"He—he's *gone*!" gasped Abbott. "Don't stand there gaping! Do something!"

"So I gathered," said Dawlish. He finished. "I'll be ready in three minutes. Ask for Room Thirty-one on the telephone, will you; someone was supposed to be watching the suite during the night."

By the time Freddie answered the telephone sleepily, Dawlish had finished washing and was knotting his tie.

"Here—here he is," Abbott said, in a hushed voice.

Dawlish took the receiver. "Hold on a minute, Freddie," he said, and then looked at Abbott. "When did you discover this?"

"Only ten minutes ago. *Less* than ten minutes ago. I came straight here."

"When did you last see him?"

"It was about half past four," gasped Abbott; "I thought I heard something and went to see if he had called me, but he was in bed then, I saw him."

"That's a help," said Dawlish, and spoke into the receiver again. "Freddie, did anything happen on your watch?"

"Good lord, no, old boy. Dull as ditchwater. What's up?"

"Galloway's flown. Did you stay there all the time?"

"Why, yes, I—" There was a pause, and then a gasp of shocked horror from Freddie. "I say, old boy, I'm *terribly* sorry. I did dip for a few minutes. Hared down to my room for a quick one. As a matter of fact I was gone practically *seven* minutes. Pat, you aren't serious, are you?"

"I'm afraid so," said Dawlish, "but I don't know that it means much yet. He might have gone of his own accord."

"He didn't!" cried Abbott.

"Anyhow, call Tim, get dressed and come along to Galloway's room, will you?" said Dawlish to Freddie. He rang off. "Are you quite sure he didn't go of his own accord?" he asked Abbott, hopefully.

"But why should he? He had planned to drive out as far as Chilham Beach this morning."

"Have you told the police?"

"Of course I haven't. You're supposed to look after him, aren't you? It's your fault. I always knew you were phoney; I always knew—"

"Let's get along to his room," said Dawlish.

The bed had been slept in, but was not badly rumpled. There were no signs of a struggle. Abbott, calmer now, went through the wardrobe, and announced that one light-brown suit was missing. It became obvious that Galloway had got up and dressed in the middle of the night, but there was no evidence to show whether he had been forced to do so. It was even possible that he would come back during the morning.

"Is anything else missing, do you know?" Dawlish asked.

"I—I haven't looked," muttered Abbott. "I don't know what to do."

He started to search the suite, breaking off when there was a ring at the door. Dawlish went to admit Tim and a dismayed Freddie, who realized that he was largely responsible.

Dawlish grinned at sight of his face.

"Cheer up, Freddie, it isn't all the world." He explained the circumstances briefly. "The question is whether to tell the police or no. I'm inclined to think yes. Abbott's right in saying that Galloway might be dead. I'll ring Longstaffe from my room. See that Abbott keeps working."

Felicity listened to his brief story in some alarm, and continued to dress while he telephoned Longstaffe. It was Sunday morning, so he rang the policeman's private number. Longstaffe soon came on the line.

"So I took my man off too soon."

"We don't know that yet," said Dawlish, reassuringly. "Galloway might have decided to pull a fast one."

"It would happen on Sunday," groaned Longstaffe.

Dawlish finished dressing, then went back to Galloway's rooms. There was a small brief-case missing, and Abbott swore that he did not know what was in it. Galloway had the only key, and Galloway had always kept important documents in the brief-case; Abbott had not been allowed to touch it.

He looked aghast when Dawlish told him that the police were coming. He was frightened; perhaps he would have to answer awkward questions. He muttered that he was not hungry when Dawlish suggested that he should go downstairs for breakfast.

By that time Muriel was up and dressed, and for the first time Tim had breakfast at the Dawlishes' table.

"This properly puts the lid on it," Tim grumbled. "If Freddie hadn't been such a fool—"

"I don't see how you can blame Freddie," said Muriel, sharply. "You might have done the same thing."

"Oh," mumbled Tim. "Sorry. Are you going back today?"

"I must," said Muriel.

"Freddie won't want to," said Dawlish. "You'll have to cheer him up on the train, Muriel."

A waiter came up. "Excuse me, sir . . ."

"Yes," said Dawlish, forcing a smile.

"Superintendent Longstaffe is in the hall, sir."

"Oh, thanks," said Dawlish, and went out of the dining-room. The moment he set eyes on Longstaffe he knew that the news was bad. Harry May was coming into the hall, and his expression was equally gloomy.

"Well?" asked Dawlish, tensely.

"We've found him," said Longstaffe. "Dead at the foot of the cliffs. Thrown over, apparently, like White." He looked at May. "You go on upstairs, Harry, and see what's going on there." Harry May hurried off and Longstaffe went to a chair and sat on the arm. "Had you any idea that this was going to happen, Dawlish?"

"I knew no more about it than you," said Dawlish. "I've told you that he hired me to look after him, and thereafter said that he needed no looking after, haven't I?"

"Yes. He wasn't scared at all, you say?"

"He didn't seem to be."

"I see," said Longstaffe. There was an odd expression in his eyes, and Dawlish wondered a little uneasily what he was thinking. "Well, there it is. I think you'd better stay on for a bit, as things have turned out."

Dawlish went back to the dining-room, conscious that Longstaffe was watching him. Longstaffe's manner had not been reassuring; the speculative look in his eyes had been almost one of suspicion.

Freddie came into the room, with a haunted look on his face.

"I've been turned out," he said. "Not worse news I hope?"

Dawlish said: "The body's at the foot of the cliffs."

Waiting for another call from the police, he wished he knew what was in Longstaffe's mind.

An hour later Longstaffe entered his office and found Inspector Davy of New Scotland Yard waiting for him. Davy did not yet know what it was about. Longstaffe told him. Davy listened to him without comment. When Longstaffe had finished, Davy looked at him, with a humorous twist to his lips.

"What's on your mind?" he demanded.

"Dawlish," said Longstaffe, briefly.

"I thought he might be. What do you think he's been up to? You don't think he murdered Galloway, do you?"

Longstaffe stirred restlessly. "I think I ought to think so," he said. "I do know there is a pretty strong chain of circumstantial evidence against him."

Davy said mildly, "All right, let's have it."

"It sticks out a mile," Longstaffe said. "In the first place, he came down here after Galloway because he had lost money and thought Galloway was responsible. Next, he was the only witness of what happened to Jonathan White. He pitched a story about two men and a car—"

"Wait a minute," interrupted Davy. "Didn't you find evidence that two other people had been near the spot? Footprints and fingerprints?"

"Oh, someone else had been there, but they might have been working with Dawlish. We didn't get fingerprints that were any good. *I* wouldn't be surprised if the men Armstrong and Jeremy were concerned. Dawlish let them get safely away, and then told his story. Isn't that feasible?"

Davy agreed that it was feasible, but showed no enthusiasm.

"I don't suggest that Dawlish set out to murder him for gain," Longstaffe said, "but he might have appointed himself a kind of Lord High Executioner. White and Galloway were not much good. He might have decided to get rid of them."

"That might possibly apply to Galloway, but how could it apply to White?" asked Davy.

"We don't know everything that Dawlish knows," said Longstaffe, sceptically. "Dawlish obviously scared Galloway. I wouldn't put it past him to have sprinkled strychnine on that sugar himself, to raise a scare so that he could get into our good graces as well as Galloway's. He could have put the stuff in White's pocket. He certainly came down here with the intention of forcing an acquaintance with Galloway, and succeeded in that all right. Galloway was obviously nervous about him. He forced Galloway to give the Kingham family a thousand pounds. He *says* Galloway willingly paid that twenty-five thousand into the absurd fund, but I have my doubts. I think he forced it out of the man, and then tried to get more. Galloway refused, and—"

"He was in a hurry, wasn't he?" asked Davy, still mildly. "Twenty-five thousand pounds in one week was surely enough even for Dawlish."

Longstaffe rubbed his chin.

"I know you don't think there's anything in it, but you're

prejudiced because you know Dawlish. Look at the facts. I took my man away from Galloway's suite two nights ago. Dawlish, on his own admission, left one of his friends there. The friend says he went to his room during his spell of duty, and in that few minutes the thing happened. Now if Dawlish and both the friends went along, took Galloway away and, when he wouldn't do what they wanted, flung him over the cliffs, that would explain the whole business, wouldn't it?"

"I suppose so," admitted Davy.

"Of course it would," snapped Longstaffe. "In my opinion Dawlish and the men ought to be held for questioning."

Davy smiled. "I shouldn't try to work on Dawlish! Even if there were anything in what you say, have you a strong enough case to pull Dawlish in?"

"It's strong enough to ask him to make a statement,"

"And he'll make one gladly," said Davy.

"You've fully made up your mind that, Dawlish is blond perfection, haven't you?" said Longstaffe, with a sneer in his voice.

Davy said soothingly: "You're upset, but I shouldn't try to take it out on Dawlish. He isn't a man to commit cold-blooded murder, and he isn't a man to kill anyone by accident and then try to cover."

"I hope you're right. *I'm* certainly not sure. You'd want to catch him red-handed before you admitted that he might be up to his eyes in crime, wouldn't you?"

Davy said blandly: "Yes, I would, old chap. Now let's get along to the morgue. The body will be there by now, won't it?"

"It should be," said Longstaffe. "The *post-mortem* had better be some time today. I suppose it's only a matter of form. Galloway went over the cliff, broke his neck and made a nasty mess of himself. Two fishermen found him."

"I suppose Galloway didn't fall by accident?" said Davy.

"Of course he didn't fall by accident; he was pushed over deliberately. Let's get along."

He drove a silent Davy to the morgue. As they turned into the street, a tall figure moved along the pavement, and Longstaffe jammed on his brakes too sharply, throwing Davy forward.

"Do you see that?"

"Dawlish on the spot," said Davy, and then added with a shade of alarm: "You haven't shown him what you suspect, have you? He'd twig it pretty quickly."

"Oh, he's too good to be true," said Longstaffe, sourly.

Dawlish greeted them with a broad smile, showing nothing of his disquiet. Longstaffe nodded distantly, and looked sour when Dawlish and Davy shook hands. Davy was deliberately formal, and neither of them asked what Dawlish was doing there.

"We'd better get in," Longstaffe said.

"Any room for a little one?" asked Dawlish.

Longstaffe stared. "I don't think there's any need for you to view the body," he said. "Abbott will identify it in due course."

"Oh," said Dawlish. "Well, that's up to you."

Davy was looking hard at Longstaffe, who shrugged his shoulders and said with ill grace that he suspected there was no reason why Dawlish should not satisfy his morbid curiosity. They went into the morgue together.

The inner room struck cold. The body lay on one of the six stone slabs, covered with a sheet. Two uniformed policemen and an attendant were present and Longstaffe motioned to one of the men, who pulled the sheet back and revealed the head and shoulders.

The man had been severely injured, and his head was at an odd angle to his body, showing clearly how he had met his death. The face was so badly disfigured that Dawlish did not immediately pick out the features. The frizzy hair was hardly touched . . .

Hardly touched! Yet Galloway must have fallen on his head or he could hardly have broken his neck. Dawlish stared more closely. He certainly could not be sure that he was looking at Galloway. There were certain features which might be Galloway's, and from what he could see of the clothes, they were the missing light-brown suit. Yet the uninjured head, after the heavy fall and the injuries to the rest of his face, really puzzled him.

"That's odd, you know," Davy said. "How did he get away with hardly a scratch on his head?"

Davy voiced the reasoning which had already passed through Dawlish's mind. Longstaffe was reluctant to follow Davy's trend of thought, until Davy came out with it broadside on.

"It wouldn't surprise me if this proved to be someone else," he said. "The face was disfigured to make identification difficult, but they forgot the head. He didn't fall down the cliff; the injuries were caused in some other way, to make it look as if he had. He was taken to that part of the shore by boat. Of course, the police-surgeon might not agree with me. I doubt whether anyone who knew Galloway will identify the body, either—if once the suspicion is sown. What do you think, Dawlish?"

Dawlish agreed that there might be something in it. Longstaffe said nothing, but looked ill-at-ease. Dawlish murmured his thanks and left them. He walked back to the hotel, quite convinced that the dead man was not Galloway. That could be construed two ways: that someone wanted Galloway presumed dead, or that Galloway himself thought he would be wise to 'die' and pop up again under a new guise.

"Which wouldn't be a bad idea at all," murmured Dawlish to himself.

CHAPTER FIFTEEN

BERESFORD ON TENTERHOOKS

Ted Beresford was a greatly worried man.

He did not like to be in London when Dawlish and the others were active at Highsea. He was displeased with himself because he had learned so little about Jonathan White. The man must have left some trace, must have had some confidant, could not have died leaving himself and his life wrapped in mystery.

These two things were in themselves more than enough to worry Beresford, but they paled into insignificance beside his, other anxiety. Until that time he had imagined that the process of childbirth was painful and uncomfortable, but always quick and on time. Even Joan's glowing face when he went to see her, twice and three times a day, failed to console him.

He sat miserably in his flat, and counted the minutes. He was due to see Joan at half past two, and it was now one-thirty. At half past eleven, when he had last seen her, she had admitted that she wasn't feeling so well, so he was now at a fever-pitch of anxiety.

The telephone rang, and he leapt to his feet and flew across the room—no mean feat, since he had one artificial leg. There was a call from Highsea for him.

"Hallo, Ted," said Dawlish, and Ted thawed. "Any home news yet?"

"Still waiting," said Ted, sadly.

"It can't be much longer," said Dawlish, encouragingly. "You haven't done anything about White this last day or two, I suppose? You haven't had time."

"I've had time," said Ted, "but it's a blank, Pat. I know there must be a line somewhere, but I can't find it. Why don't you try to come up yourself?—you might be lucky."

"I'm stuck down here for a bit longer," said Dawlish. "A man supposed to be Galloway was murdered last night, and Galloway is missing. Give Trivett a call, I'd like to know his reaction. Take the line that you're worried about me—you know I want to get to town, and can't understand what's keeping me. Will you do that?"

"Yes, but will it help?"

"It might," said Dawlish. "Tell him about the Galloway business, of course, and that I'm convinced the real Galloway is still alive."

"Right-ho," said Ted, lugubriously. "I've just got time to have a word with Trivett before I slip along to see Joan. I'll ring you back about four, Pat. I can't manage it before that."

"Four o'clock will do fine," Dawlish assured him.

Ted replaced the receiver. Immediately he telephoned Superintendent Trivett, but Trivett was out.

The telephone rang again.

A man said, "Is that Mr. Edward Beresford?"

"Yes," said Ted, at once despondent. The voice was unfamiliar.

"I believe you have been making inquiries about a Mr. Jonathan White?"

"Yes, that's right."

"On behalf of Mr. Patrick Dawlish."

"Yes," said Ted, really interested now.

"I have some information," said the man. "I am speaking from Mr. White's flat. I am his brother-in-law. I wonder if you could come and see me at once?"

"At—once?" breathed Ted, and glanced at the clock. No, it would take him half an hour at least to get to Chiswick, and in a little over half an hour he was due at the nursing-home. "I can make it about half past four," he said; "will that be all right?"

"I'm afraid I shall be gone by then," said the other, and he sounded despondent. "It can't be helped, but I did want a word with you."

"Hold on," said Ted, urgently. He did another quick mental calculation, and arrived at the same conclusion. He could not get out to Chiswick and be back in time to see Joan in the normal visiting hours. Yet this might be the line he and Pat had been tapping for a week. "I'll come, I'll be there in a little more than half an hour."

"I'm *so* glad," said the speaker.

Ted rang off, and immediately put in a call to the nursing-home. A nurse answered. She laughed when he asked whether it would matter if he were late. "No," she said, "I'm quite sure it won't."

"But my wife's expecting me," Ted told her, "will you tell her that I have been unavoidably delayed, but I'll be along before five?"

"Yes, Mr. Beresford, don't worry."

"Thanks," said Ted, and rang off.

He hurried downstairs, where his Lagonda was waiting. He checked the petrol and started out for Chiswick.

He pulled up outside Hollway Mansions, a small block of flats. Ted went up to the first floor, using the automatic lift. He reached Flat 17 and rang the bell. There was no answer.

He scowled fiercely. "If this is a hoax," he muttered. He rang and knocked at the same time, thinking of the lost hour with Joan.

A man passed along the passage, looking at him curiously.

A change came over Beresford as the stranger disappeared. For the first time he realized that he was working on a mystery which had already led to murder, and—he was making a complete fool of himself.

He rang again. He was conscious of watching eyes.

As he rang yet again, he heard clearly a man's voice, saying: "*Hurry up!*"

So someone was inside the flat. Swiftly he considered what would be the best course of action. Probably it would be wisest to go away, watch and follow anyone who eventually left the flat.

New sounds came from the flat. He turned softly on his heels. "*Mr. Beresford.*"

A gentle whisper came from farther along the passage. Yet he could see no one. Then Beresford saw the last door in the passage standing ajar. A man's face appeared for a moment, then disappeared. He went towards it.

Beresford heard another door open farther along the passage. It was of White's flat. Then the whisper, and the door opposite him opened again. He stepped inside. It was the only thing to do if he wanted to avoid being seen by the people in White's flat.

A little man was staring up at him, dressed in clerical grey and wearing a black tie. His expression had a funeral air.

"I'm—I'm sorry to be so mysterious, Mr. Beresford."

Not quite a dwarf, he was small enough to be unusual. His pale, heart-shaped face was remarkable only for enormous brown eyes, with dark patches beneath them.

"Listen," he said. "They might come here."

The big man and the small waited tensely, holding their

breath. Someone walked along the passage. The small man's fingers tightened on Beresford's arm. The footsteps drew nearer, and then stopped—*outside.*

The little man drew in a long, hissing breath.

The footsteps receded. A door closed as two men spoke. Then there was silence.

"Thank heavens!" gasped the little man, and Beresford saw that his forehead was beaded with perspiration. "I was afraid they had seen you come in here," he said; "they—they frighten me so much."

"There isn't as much as all that to worry about, you know."

"I assure you there *is* a great deal to worry about."

"Supposing you tell me what it's all about?" asked Beresford.

"Well, they murdered *him,*" the little man said.

"Do you mean Jonathan White?"

"Yes, of course I do. He—he was my brother-in-law. I married his sister. Thank heavens Beaty's away! I think this would drive her mad, I do really. But Jonathan's death was such a shock to his mother—she's very old you know, nearly eighty—it made her ill. Beaty hurried down to look after her, because you can't rely on servants nowadays, and so I'm here on my own. That— that's one of the things that frightens me. If Beaty were here, I wouldn't feel half so bad; she gives me confidence." He drew a deep breath, and—Beresford marvelled at the sight—there were tears in his eyes. "A wonderful wife. My—my name's Henderson. I ought to start from the beginning, oughtn't I?"

"It would be helpful," said Beresford.

"Well—I'll do my best," said Henderson. "It all started a long time ago, of course, before poor Jonathan's murder. I didn't know anything about it, except that Jonathan *was* frightened. That was a little while after the *Hedshire Estates* affair. Poor Jonathan was very hard hit. And soon afterwards, when he wrote to Mr. Galloway and told him what he thought of him, he became frightened. I could see it. I didn't ask him anything about it, for he was always one to keep himself to himself, but there it was. And then, a fortnight ago, he told me that he was frightened because he was going to try to do some good to the people who had lost in *Hedshires,* and he was afraid of what Galloway would do."

"I see," said Ted, who did not see at all.

"Well, it was the kind of thing I would expect of Jonathan," went on Henderson, "but it wasn't fair for him to be worried nearly out of his life. I—I was in his office one evening, and he had two visitors. Unpleasant, uncouth fellows. Jonathan dealt with them very firmly. They wanted him to stop meddling—that's the term they used—with *Hedshires.* They became threatening and they frightened me, but Jonathan did not let them see that they also frightened him. Am I making it all clear, Mr. Beresford?"

"Very clear," said Ted.

"I'm so glad. I am doing my very best. Well, the next day Jonathan said that he was going to see Galloway himself, and have it out with him. He went down to Highsea, and the next thing *I* knew, he was dead. I hadn't any doubt that this man Galloway was responsible. Have you, Mr. Beresford? Don't you think Galloway arranged it?"

"He might have done," said Beresford, cautiously.

"I haven't any doubt at all," repeated Henderson. "Well, I mustn't run on. The truth is, Mr. Beresford, that the police have been here, asking a lot of questions, and there was one thing I had to keep back from them. Jonathan said to me, he said, just before he went: 'There's a chance that a man named Dawlish will do something for the *Hedshire* people,' he said, 'and if he is doing anything, you can tell *him* about this, but don't let anyone else know.' Well, I am a very precise man," went on

Henderson, "and I asked Jonathan if it would be all right for me to tell *friends* of Mr. Dawlish, and he said 'yes'. That's why I knew about you. I knew you were making inquiries; you'd been here once or twice before, the people next door told me. And then—*they* reappeared."

"Whom do you mean by 'they'?"

"The two men who had tried to frighten Jonathan," said Henderson. "They called this morning, made me go into Jonathan's flat, and started asking me questions. I don't mind admitting that they frightened me out of my life, but they went off and I foxed them." For the first time Henderson showed some sign of real animation. "I didn't tell them anything."

"What did they want to know?"

"Why, the thing Jonathan told me and that I wasn't to tell the police," said Henderson. "Of course, you want to know what it is," went on Henderson, naïvely. "Well, this is it: Jonathan had bought *thousands* of *Hedshire* shares for a little or nothing. Two shillings each, I think he paid. He said he couldn't stand by and see people ruined, and if two shillings a share would help them, then he would gladly buy them and try to make some arrangement with Galloway afterwards. He left the shares with me, you see, before he went to Highsea. I've got them here. That's why those two men frightened me so much. Oh—I forgot."

Beresford was thinking, with much satisfaction, that he had found what Pat and the police had been looking for.

"Yes, I forgot—those men *made* me telephone you. I understood that they wanted to ask you how much Dawlish knows. I knew they intended to wait there for you. Then someone telephoned them, and they had to go. They locked me in one of the rooms, and what they didn't know was that Jonathan had left the spare keys of his rooms with me, and I had them in my pocket. So I got out. I didn't go back to my own flat. I know the people here very well, you see, and the people in this flat were going out after lunch, so I asked them if I could use it for a very special reason, and they said I could. Well-then I saw these men come back and go into the flat—Jonathan's flat. They must have had a shock when they found me gone! I waited here, and called you. I thought you'd never hear me."

"I was slow," admitted Beresford. "Do you think they've looked into your flat?"

"Oh, I expect so. They must be angry; I've certainly foxed *them*."

"Oh, yes," said Beresford, "you've done remarkably well. But didn't you say the shares were here?" he added.

"Oh, I didn't mean *here*," said Henderson, apologetically, "I meant in my flat. That's two doors away."

"And these two men want them?"

"Oh, yes, that's what they're after. I won't tell you what they threatened, but it was something horrible, if I didn't tell them where to find them, but I convinced them that I didn't know. They're safe enough in my flat, I've got a safe."

"Yes," said Beresford, and he meant 'no'. He got up quickly, and Henderson stared at him in surprise. "I'm just a little worried, though, in case they're searching your flat now."

Henderson's voice rose. "Searching my flat!"

"That kind of person does do that kind of thing," said Beresford, gravely. "I'll hop along and find out if there is anyone inside, shall I?"

CHAPTER SIXTEEN

LOW CUNNING

Henderson hopped from one foot to the other, in such distress that Beresford wondered, for the first time, whether it was genuine.

"What is your flat number?"

"Fifteen," said Henderson. "This is Thirteen; mine is next door but one, a *little* nearer to poor Jonathan's."

"You stay here," said Beresford, "and let me have your key."

"No, *please*. I feel that this is my responsibility—"

"It's your responsibility to keep safe," Beresford told him. "You're a witness of some importance. Don't worry, they won't take too many risks, and I may be wrong about them searching your room."

Henderson handed over the key, but he looked miserable.

Beresford stepped into the passage along to Flat 15 and paused outside the door. The door of Jonathan White's flat remained closed.

Beresford listened intently.

There *were* sounds of movement in Henderson's flat!

He waited for a few moments to make sure, and then smiled

broadly. Here were the 'bad men', delivered into his hands! He inserted the key carefully. He pushed the door open gently and stepped inside. Now the sounds of movement and of voices were much clearer, and he heard a scratching sound. He fancied that one of the intruders was trying to open a locked drawer.

The lay-out of the flat was exactly the same as the one he had just left. The door leading to the sitting-room was ajar, and as Beresford went towards it a shadow appeared. Beresford stood with his hands a little in front of him, prepared for someone to come out. The shadow disappeared, and one of the men said:

"The safe's the thing all right."

"We can't get it open," said the other.

"Then well have to take it with us."

"What, *that* weight? We'd never carry it!"

"We'll have to carry it."

Beresford opened the door a little farther and peered inside.

The men were in a far corner of the room, standing by an office safe. It was fairly large, standing as high as the waist of the smaller of the two men in front of it.

They bent down and tried to get their hands beneath to ease it up, but they failed to move the safe an inch.

"I told you," said the shorter man, sourly.

"Shut up," said the other. "We want something to lever it up with, that's all."

"We ought to wait for Henderson, and get the keys from him," said the smaller man, "and I—"

"I wonder if I can help," said Beresford, in a cooing voice.

They jumped and spun round. Open-mouthed, they gaped at him. It now seemed certain that White's brother-in-law was all that he claimed to be.

"After all," said Beresford, "I'm a big, strong man. A little safe like that shouldn't give me any trouble."

Neither of the men spoke.

"I do hope I haven't scared you."

"How did you get in?"

"I walked in," said Beresford. "You're not the only specialists in opening doors. Now, about that safe. Why do you want it?" He saw that the smaller of the men was sliding his hands towards his coat pocket. He waited until the man had actually dipped his fingers into his pocket, and then shot out his arm. He snatched the man's hand away; a small automatic was hanging from unsteady fingers. He shook it free and thrust the man away from him.

Beresford swept his right arm round. The leader of the burglars staggered back against the wall, feeling as if a tornado had hit him. His gun, too, fell from his grasp, and they lay near each other on the floor. Beresford picked them up.

There was a telephone on a table near the window, and Beresford went towards it. "Scotland Yard, now—that's Whitehall 1212, isn't it?" He began to dial. "I will call the police, unless you can offer some compensation. What will you tell me if I do let you go?" he added, and paused in his dialling.

"Ken, tell him!" burst out of the smaller man.

Beresford saw one of them look towards the door and start, as if someone were there.

He beamed. "No, that's an old one," he said. "Let me start asking questions. What did you want from the safe?"

"*Hedshire Estates* stock, I expect," said a voice behind him. "That's what they usually want."

Beresford stiffened, in startled amazement. The two men in front of him had transferred their fear from him to the newcomer. Beresford felt sick with disappointment and self-disgust. Not for a moment had he dreamed that the expressions on the men's faces meant that someone *had* come in—but there was the man, behind him.

Beresford did not turn round.

"Don't you think that's likely?" the man asked him.

He had a soft, lilting voice, and he sounded amused. Beresford resisted the temptation to look round. He heard a footstep. A man appeared on a level with him, but out of range of his long arms. There was another sound, and someone appeared on the other side. One man was tall, fair-haired and smiling. The other was short and stocky, heavy-featured, nearly bald.

The fair-haired man spoke, and thus identified himself as the man with the lilting voice.

"This is too bad, Beresford, isn't it? You thought you were the only possessor of low cunning. I shouldn't do anything foolish. I don't want to hurt you; all I want is to get that safe open. Where's Henderson?" he asked of the stocky man, who simply jerked his thumb towards the door.

"He didn't make any trouble, I hope," said the fair-haired man, in that cooing voice.

The stocky man shook his head.

"That's good," said the fair-haired man, and stood in front of Beresford, smiling broadly. He was a good-looking fellow in the middle thirties. He completely ignored 'Ken' and his companion, who had neither moved nor spoken since his arrival. "Look after them," he said, and inclined his head slightly towards the men behind him.

The stocky man spoke for the first time.

"Turn round," he said, simply.

Beresford concentrated on assessing the situation and the men involved. One thing seemed obvious: the original burglars knew the fair-haired man and his companion, and were afraid of them. They seemed to have every justification for their fear. It was seldom that a man succeeded in unnerving Beresford, but the fair-haired man was well on the way towards doing that.

Both the short dark men 'turned round'.

Then Beresford witnessed an astonishing thing. The stocky man moved with bewildering speed. He took something from his pocket—a cosh, a weapon of weighted leather. He brought it down on the heads of the two dark men. Only one blow was needed for each victim. They were knocked out on their feet, and fell heavily. The stocky man skipped aside, to avoid one of them, and then turned and looked at the fair-haired fellow, whose smile had never left his face and who had watched Beresford closely all the time.

"We're efficient, aren't we?" he said.

"Very," said Beresford.

"We can do even better," said the fair-haired man. "Would you like to know what happened?"

"That's up to you," said Beresford.

"Well, we watched," said the fair-haired man, sounding pleased with himself. "We knew that you and the police were after Henderson, and we felt quite sure that he had information of value to us. So, we watched. And when those two idiots arrived, we knew that *one* attempt was being made to force Henderson's hand. Then you came. We thought—or should I say *I* thought—that you would deal with them and then we would deal with you. It's worked out very well. But you find it somewhat puzzling. I don't blame you. You see, I work for one interested party and they work for another. Both parties want the same thing—*Hedshire Estates* stock. After you had left Henderson, we visited him. He's a frightened little customer, isn't he?"

"Why frighten him?" asked Beresford.

"I rather like dealing with frightened men," said the fair-haired fellow, his smile broadening. "They're so much more amenable than those who are less easily scared. I would have some difficulty in making *you* talk, I've no doubt, but Henderson—ah, here he is. Come in, Henderson. We won't hurt you if you do what you're told."

Beresford felt really sorry for Henderson.

"Now, Henderson, give me the key to the safe."

Beresford expected Henderson to submit without a word of protest. He was agreeably surprised when the man drew back.

Henderson gasped, "Mr. Beresford, don't let them take anything away!"

The fair-haired man said: "Beresford can't help himself. Hand over the key or you'll get hurt."

"I won't—I *won't!*" screeched Henderson. He jumped forward, and the fair-haired man backed away in alarm, a victim of his own cocksureness. The stocky man moved into the attack, and the other who had been guarding Henderson jumped forward.

They had reckoned without Beresford.

He swept his right arm round and took great pleasure in hitting the stocky man on the side of the jaw. Then he swung round towards the fair-haired man. Had he had the normal use of his legs he would have turned the tables without difficulty, but he was slow because of his false leg. The split-second that he lost enabled the fair-haired man to get out of his way.

Henderson had spun round and was rushing towards the door, with only one man after him, for the stocky man was still dazed. Beresford got his balance back and faced the fair-haired man, only to find that he held an automatic; his expression suggested that he would not hesitate to use it.

"Keep away, Beresford!"

Beresford hesitated.

There was a squeal from the door, high-pitched, as if someone had been badly hurt. Beresford turned his head, in spite of his own danger. Henderson lay on the floor, his face distorted, and the man who had brought him in kicked him in the groin. Henderson turned deathly white, and groaned. The assailant drew back his foot again.

"That's enough," said the fair-haired man. "Get the key from him." He looked steadily at Beresford. "You won't be so lucky if you play the fool again. Move back against the wall."

Beresford obeyed, because of the gun.

The man who had kicked Henderson came forward with a bunch of keys. The fair-haired fellow nodded towards the safe. As the keys were being tried, the stocky man picked himself up and stood rubbing his chin. Beresford expected to find malevolence in the thug's eyes. Instead, there was a look almost of admiration.

"You pack *some* punch, Guv'nor."

The look of admiration lingered in the thug's eyes.

The man by the safe turned his head.

"Got it," he said, and pulled the door open.

"See if they're there," said the fair-haired man. The man at the safe took out a number of papers, followed by some unsealed foolscap envelopes. He extracted the contents. There were several small red books, and a number of share certificates.

"Okay," said the man, after a brief glance.

"How many?"

The man made a quick calculation, "About ten thousand."

"There should be more," said the fair-haired man. "You don't know how many he's got, Beresford, do you?"

Beresford shook his head.

"Wait a minute," said the man by the safe, "there's some more." He took out another foolscap envelope, and his face brightened as he glanced at them. "Total of forty-nine thousand," he declared; "is that all right?"

"*That's* better," said the fair-haired man. "That's all I expected.

Forty-nine thousand *Hedshire Estates* shares for nothing, Beresford; that's not bad, is it?"

"Are they worth anything?" asked Beresford.

He was astonished at the man's reaction. At first he looked startled; then he began to laugh.

"Well, well, *well*!" exclaimed the fair-haired man at last. "Are they *worth* anything! Dawlish isn't as clever as I thought . . ." He paused, and a look of genuine bewilderment crossed his face. "Do you mean that Dawlish doesn't *know?*"

Beresford did what Dawlish would have done in those circumstances, and said firmly that neither he nor Dawlish had any idea what the man was talking about.

"Then why is he working on this?" asked the fair-haired man. "That story of trying to recoup the losses of all the fools who lost money—*that's* not the truth, is it?"

Beresford said, "You wouldn't understand it, would you?"

"No, I certainly wouldn't. I don't believe anyone would take the risks Dawlish is taking for the sake of people he doesn't know." He still looked bewildered. "Dawlish hasn't told you, that's what it amounts to, I suppose. Maybe that's as well." He laughed again, "Got them all, Frazer?" Frazer, it appeared, was the man at the safe, and he nodded. "Good. We'll clear out."

He nodded at Beresford.

That was a signal, for the stocky man said in a curiously mild voice, "Turn round."

"Oh," said Beresford. "It's my turn, is it?"

Henderson still lay in silent agony.

"Sorry, Guv'nor," said the stocky man, and really seemed regretful. "I've got to lay you out for a few minutes. It won't hurt—much."

As he spoke a whistle came from outside, the thug turned and said one word: "Police."

That was all, but it brought new life to Beresford, and it scared the fair-haired man and Frazer. They hurried towards the door. The men went out of the room and closed the door. Beresford moved quickly towards it, but heard the key turn in the lock.

Then he heard a shout outside—and the roar of a shot followed. There were thumping noises. Beresford launched himself at the door. It resisted the first onslaught but gave way at the second.

Another shot roared out.

He heard cries of alarm from all over the building, and the sound of thudding and of running feet grew louder. He staggered into the hall. The passage door was wide open. As he reached it he saw a policeman stretched out on the floor, clutching at his chest. Another was reeling back from a blow from the thug, who was the only one of the three assailants in sight. Two other policemen were between the thug and the stairs.

Beresford stepped forward.

The thug took three quick steps and then launched himself at both policemen, his arms whirling like flails, the cosh still held in one hand. He moved too quickly for Beresford to do anything, and his rush carried the policemen off their feet. He reached the stairs and raced down them, while doors opened, men and women called out and then a woman screamed.

CHAPTER SEVENTEEN

DAWLISH COMES TO TOWN

Beresford got downstairs as quickly as he could. By the time he reached the hall the thug was standing a few yards in front of a policeman, cosh in one hand. From somewhere along the road came the sound of a car engine.

The thug jumped.

The policeman closed with him courageously enough, but went down beneath the first onslaught. Then a car came in sight. A small touring car, with the hood down, and the fair-haired man at the wheel. It was travelling at thirty miles an hour at least. The thug took a flying leap, managed to get a hold and, as the car disappeared round a corner, clambered into the back.

Beresford felt almost glad that he had got away, but he felt very differently about the fair-haired man and Frazer, who had kicked Henderson.

An hour later, Beresford telephoned Dawlish. It was then a little before four o'clock. Dawlish sounded cheerful enough, and asked at once:

"Boy or girl, Ted?"

"What?" said Ted, blankly.

"I said—"

"Great Scott!" exploded Ted, in sudden dismay. "Good lord! I—I've actually *forgotten* . . . I never would have believed it—just a moment." Ted turned to Trivett. "I say old chap, ring the nursing-home for me, will you? Ask them how things are. Mayfair 07133—got it?" Trivett nodded and picked up another telephone. "I still can't believe it—to forget Joan. Someone—I don't know who—got away with forty-nine thousand *Hedshire Estates* shares. White had given them to his brother-in-law to look after. The brother-in-law had a nasty time, but he's not badly hurt. I'm sitting with Trivett just now; he thinks you might like to come up for a few hours."

"I would," said Dawlish, "but the Highsea Police seem determined to keep me here."

"Oh, I expect he can fix it," said Beresford. "Can't you, Bill?" He looked at Trivett, who was speaking on the other telephone. "Bill," he repeated.

"*Hush!*" exclaimed Trivett, with a strained look on his face. Into the telephone he said: "Yes—yes—how much?—eight and three quarters—what a beauty! Yes, I'll tell him."

"*Pat!*" roared Beresford. "It's arrived. Hold on! Bill, give me that telephone!" He snatched at it. "Hallo, hallo, Nurse-Sister—*Matron!*" He looked up at Trivett with a horrified expression. "They've rung off," he said, in a ghost of a voice—"they've gone."

"Congratulations, Ted," said Trivett, equably. "A son and heir."

"A—*boy*?" whispered Ted. "But how's Joan?"

"Fine! She can see you any time after half past five."

Beresford sat back, dazedly, and then a smile dawned on his face, and he lifted the other telephone. "Pat, are you still there? . . . Listen, a *boy*. . . . Yes. . . . Oh, thanks, old chap, thanks a million. . . . She's fine, Bill says; I'm going to see her at half past five." He replaced the receiver with great deliberation, oblivious of Dawlish's urgent "Hold on!"

Trivett laughed. "Is Dawlish coming up?"

"I did say something to him about it, and he said he would if he could. I gathered there's a spot of bother with the local police."

Beresford then allowed himself to be ushered out of the room. Trivett went with him and saw him into his car, and then returned to the office.

Trivett ran through the reports which he already had from Highsea. The latest had been delivered by hand that afternoon, and Davy made it clear that Longstaffe suspected that Dawlish was directly involved in the murders.

Trivett found nothing surprising in that suspicion. He had worked on practically every case in which Dawlish had been engaged, and if ever a man asked for trouble Dawlish had. His directness was refreshing, and he certainly obtained results, but he seemed almost oblivious at times to the rights of the police. The evidence which Longstaffe had produced was certainly disturbing.

He had a high regard for Dawlish. He would, however, have to get the Assistant Commissioner's approval to make a firm request to Longstaffe not to hamper Dawlish's movements.

The Assistant Commissioner, Sir Archibald Morely, was a distant relative of Dawlish's. For that reason he was inclined to be more strict and severe with Dawlish than he might otherwise have been.

Morely came in in the middle of Trivett's deliberations. Tall, dark, looking older than his forty-odd years because the top of his head was bald, he was in no very good humour; even the Assistant Commissioner of New Scotland Yard expected his Sunday afternoons to be free.

Trivett had arranged for tea to be served as soon as Morely arrived.

"Well, what is your assessment of the situation?" Morely asked, twenty minutes later. "Dawlish has been taking too much into his own hands again; that's a foregone conclusion."

Trivett smiled. "I'm not too sure that it is, this time," he said. "Dawlish doesn't usually maintain a lie, you know, and he declares that he was interested in Galloway, but that he knew nothing else until the attempt was made by White—presumably—to poison the man. As for my assessment of the situation . . ." He hesitated, and then said deliberately: "It is increasingly obvious that the *Hedshire Estates* business was deliberately engineered, and it appears likely that Galloway, the man White and perhaps a third party thought it likely that further profit could be made out of the affair. I am having further inquiries put in hand immediately about the land which was bought, because if the *Estates* are going to regain their value, it must mean that the reports that the land was worthless were wrong. If wrong survey reports and prospectuses were produced, *that's* a criminal offence, and we've got them."

"Who?"

"Galloway, for one. The Highsea police-surgeon confirms Davy's opinion that the dead man is not Galloway, and the secretary, Abbott, refuses to identify the man. There are no known relatives, but we're having a friend of Galloway's go down to Highsea to look at the body. My personal opinion is that Galloway found things getting too hot for him, decided to buy Dawlish off and so gain time, gained it, made his preparations, and then disappeared. We'll probably find him, but before we can look properly we must establish the fact that he had been criminally implicated."

"Can you?" asked Morely.

"I don't know. We can establish that White was buying up these shares. His brother-in-law, Henderson, is guilty of keeping material facts from us, but I don't know whether we've a case. Galloway's part in the affair isn't criminal, so far as we can say. He might be implicated in the murder of the man who looked like him and he may employ some of the people who have committed crimes, but we're sure of nothing against him yet."

"Who else might be involved?"

"Leaving Dawlish out of the reckoning for a moment," Trivett said, "we have three possibilities: first, Jonathan White, Henderson and, possibly, other partners working with him. With White dead and Henderson frightened out of his life, I think we ought to forget them for the moment. Then, Galloway *might* have employed this fair-haired man I told you about on the telephone. There was the fair-haired man, another called Frazer and the third, a strong-arm man for whom Beresford appears to have some esteem."

"The trouble with all Dawlish's friends is that they've no sense of moral values," Morely growled.

"You're partly right there, sir," agreed Trivett, with his tongue in his cheek. "But to complete the picture—Galloway *was* once nearly murdered, and his room at the Marine Hotel—as I now understand—was once burglariously entered. The fair-haired man might be responsible for the attacks on Galloway. That would leave a different set-up, wouldn't it?"

"Three different groups of people after the *Hedshire Estates* shares?" said Morely, unconvinced.

"It's possible," Trivett said, "and it's also possible that Galloway was actually kidnapped. If this fair-haired man is working for him, then we can assume that Galloway vanished of his own free will, being afraid of what Dawlish or we might find out about him. If the fair-haired man is Galloway's enemy, then he may have kidnapped Galloway, put in the stooge body at Highsea to try to hoodwink us, and still be holding the real Galloway to some form of ransom."

"I see," said Morely, and brooded for a few moments. Then he asked grudgingly, "What's Dawlish's view on all this?"

"I'm not quite sure, and I'd like to talk to him. But there's a difficulty. Understandably enough, the Highsea Police want to keep him down there. I don't like *ordering* them to let him travel to London, and Davy says that Longstaffe isn't in a mood to listen to reason."

"Nonsense!" said Morely. "Dawlish hasn't been charged, there's no reason at all why he shouldn't go where he wants to."

"But Dawlish will make things worse for himself if he comes to London after Longstaffe has made a pointed request for him to stay at Highsea," said Trivett. "I did wonder, sir, if you would have a word with Longstaffe's Chief Constable. A friendly word would make a lot of difference."

Morely raised an eyebrow. "I see," he said, gruffly. "All right. But we mustn't get this thing out of proportion, you know. As far as we are concerned at the moment, the most important immediate issue is the attack on our men this afternoon. Have you found any trace of the assailants?"

"The car was found, smashed up, near Wimbledon," Trivett told him. "We're going over it for prints, of course. Beresford has given us good descriptions of the men, and we've a general call out for them already, but we've no direct clue yet."

"All right," said Morely. "What's the telephone number of Longstaffe's chief?"

Longstaffe did not like it, but his Chief Constable had given the word. He came to the Marine Hotel in person. Dawlish felt some sympathy, for Longstaffe was a worried man.

Dawlish, Felicity and Muriel were sitting on the front lawn. Tim Jeremy and Freddie were upstairs, packing, for it had been agreed that both of them should return to London and give Beresford a hand.

Dawlish waved to an empty deck-chair.

Longstaffe accepted a cigarette. "Dawlish, I've often asked you this before. Do you know *anything* more than you've told me?"

Dawlish said, "Nothing." That was now strictly true. Since the death of the man who looked like Galloway, he had filled in the details of his story. Dawlish had not, of course, gone into details about the decisions of the Council of War.

Longstaffe grumbled, "Well, I don't seem to have enough justification for asking you to stay down here."

Dawlish laughed, in sudden good humour. "I'm glad I'm free to move again; I've an urge to go to London."

"Yes, the scene's shifted," said Longstaffe. "I rather wish *I* could come with you. Well, I needn't worry you any more now, but if you ever come back to Highsea, look out."

They shook hands. Longstaffe made off.

"Fel, we've got to pack! And we won't go back by train, we'll go by road, we can all get in the car at a pinch."

It was a little after eight o'clock when they arrived in London. Dawlish had driven at speed, earning mild protests from Tim Jeremy, but none from Freddie or Muriel. Dawlish and Felicity always stayed with Tim when they were in London, for they lived out of town.

The earlier impression that Muriel and Freddie were smitten with each other was strengthened on the journey. They drove towards Tim's flat, discussing plans for the night. Dawlish was against Muriel going to her own small flat. Freddie was equally averse to it. Muriel did not greatly mind.

"I've got it," said Felicity. "Muriel can stay with me at Tim's, and you and Freddie can make shift at Ted's."

The car pulled up outside Tim Jeremy's Brook Street flat. Beresford lived round the corner, in Jermyn Street. A little stiff after the journey, they made their way up the stairs.

"Where shall we feed, old chap?" asked Freddie.

"We'll have something sent up from the restaurant," said Dawlish. Tim was putting his key in the front door; Dawlish and Felicity were standing together just behind him; Freddie and Muriel were behind them in turn.

The landing was dark, although it was full daylight outside. It was quiet, too, and the noise of the key grating in the lock seemed loud.

There was another sound.

Dawlish heard it first, and knew that someone was lurking in the shadows of the landing.

The door opened, and daylight streamed through from the hall. Dawlish appeared to notice nothing, but ushered Felicity in and called, "After you, Muriel." Muriel stepped forward into the hall, with Freddie bringing up the rear.

Dawlish saw the crouching man in a corner, a man with a gun in his hand.

The man fired.

Dawlish swept his right arm round a split second before the shot, struck Muriel across the chest and sent her staggering back. Freddie's exclamation of astonishment was drowned in the roar of the shot. The flash lit up the face of the man with the gun. Freddie swung round and leapt at him, and the man fired again.

Freddie gasped and staggered back.

The man with the gun jumped towards the stairs, with Dawlish after him and Tim coming out of the flat at the double.

CHAPTER EIGHTEEN

ATTEMPTED TO MURDER WHOM?

The assailant moved very quickly, but Dawlish reached the next landing only a little way behind him. The man turned and fired. Dawlish, ready for it, put a hand on the banisters and vaulted over. The bullet missed both him and Tim, who was at the top of the stairs.

Dawlish landed on the last flight, and the man with the gun was between him and Tim. Dawlish went forward, knowing that he might be shot. But the sight of the big man lunging towards him, and a sudden yell from Tim, unnerved him. He fired wildly and wide; and then Dawlish reached him, and he crashed down, the gun spinning out of his hand.

Tim came up. "All right, Pat?"

"Yes, thanks." Dawlish got to his feet and looked down at the gunman, who was conscious but had suffered badly in that brief encounter. "Get him upstairs. How's Freddie?"

"I don't know."

"What a ruddy business it is!" growled Dawlish, as Tim lugged the man to his feet and half carried, half pushed him up the stairs. "It's bigger than I thought, and they're a darned sight brighter than I hoped."

On the landing Muriel was bending over Freddie, who was pale, but smiling.

"Where did it get him?" asked Dawlish.

"I'm all right," protested Freddie; "don't make a fuss, old boy. Shoulder, and missed the bone, I'd say. My lucky night." He beamed at Muriel, who looked up, tense-faced.

"Felicity's sent for a doctor," she said.

"Good—and the police?"

"I don't know," said Muriel. She looked back at Freddie, and Dawlish needed no more telling that during their brief acquaintance they had fallen deeply in love. "Can we—can we move him?" she demanded.

"I don't see why not," said Dawlish. "Let me have a look at you, Freddie." He went down on one knee and felt gently, getting his fingers wet with blood. As far as he could judge, Freddie was right—the bullet had gone through the fleshy part of the shoulder, near the armpit, but there seemed little chance that it had missed a bone. "Get a bed ready," he said, and lifted his friend effortlessly.

Felicity was coming away from the telephone. She went first and turned down the bed. Dawlish went into the bathroom for scissors, and came back to cut the sleeve away.

Felicity came in with warm water and towels. "Dr. Rolling is coming," she said, "and I've told Scotland Yard."

Dawlish examined the wound more closely, and came to the conclusion that Freddie had come off surprisingly well. The bullet had gone clean through; perhaps the bone had been missed after all. He was trying to assess the importance of everything that had happened.

Muriel said, "What do you make of it?"

"He'll be all right," Dawlish said. "Rolling won't be long." He smiled at her, and then nodded to Felicity, who went out with him, leaving Muriel with Freddie. For the first time Dawlish gave full attention to the man who had caused the trouble. He was smallish, with a nondescript face, and he was now badly frightened. He was standing by the window, and Ted was staring at him from the depths of an arm-chair.

Dawlish spoke as if the assailant were not present.

"You know what this means, don't you?"

"I wish I did," said Felicity, pushing her fingers through her hair.

"They wanted to kill Muriel," said Dawlish.

"It looked to me as if they didn't mind whom they killed, provided they got someone," said Tim, and cast a cold glance at the man by the window. "Why not have a go at him before the police arrive?"

Dawlish said: "We may, yet. You're wrong, you know. He had one purpose: to kill Muriel. If he'd just wanted to scare us, or cause alarm and despondency, he would have crept behind us, then fired, and had every chance of getting well away. He waited until the door was open and the light was good, and he also waited for Muriel." He swung round on the man in the window, gripped the man's shoulder tightly, and snapped, *"Didn't you?"*

The man gasped in fear and pain, for Dawlish's grip was vice-like. He gasped: "Yes, I—"

Felicity watched Dawlish; it was never possible to judge how he would act.

His voice grew deep. "So you were sent to kill Miss Lancing?"

The gunman did not speak.

"Why waste time?" asked Dawlish. "You've admitted it." He tightened his hold. His powerful fingers bit deeply into the man's shoulder. *"Isn't that true?"* His pressure grew tighter. "Who sent you?"

The man gasped.

Dawlish suddenly released him, then pushed him against the wall. The man staggered forward, and Dawlish gripped his shoulder again, showing no mercy. "Who sent you? Galloway?"

There was pain on the man's face, pain and fear—and, at the mention of the name Galloway, perhaps the slightest change, showing dismay. It was in no way conclusive. Dawlish released him again because there was a ring at the front-door bell.

The bedroom door opened and Muriel appeared. "Is that the doctor?" she demanded.

Felicity hurried to the door. It was Rolling.

Dawlish explained briefly. Rolling nodded, as if it were an everyday affair, and Muriel and Felicity led him into the bedroom. The door closed. Dawlish turned to look at the man who had fired the gun. Tim stood up slowly.

"Do you want any help?" he demanded.

"Probably," said Dawlish.

They stood towering over the man. He stared at Dawlish's hand, as if in fear of another terrible grip. Dawlish was thinking only of getting as much information out of the man as he could before the police arrived.

Dawlish put his hand out slowly, the fingers spread open. The other man's fear grew into terror. He drew in his breath, there was no escape. Dawlish put his hand on his shoulder and, without pressing very hard, said slowly:

"Who sent you to kill Miss Lancing?"

The man licked his lips.

Dawlish squeezed, and brought a squeal of pain from the man's lips; and then, quite unexpectedly, the man closed his eyes and slid to the floor.

"Pull him up," snapped Tim, "he's foxing."

"I'm afraid he isn't," said Dawlish, resignedly. "He just can't take it, and that means we just can't make it."

Tim glowered down on the unconscious man. "Aren't you going to look through his pockets?"

"Yes," said Dawlish, and suited the action to the word.

He was quite sure that the attack had been intended only for Muriel. It seemed likely that the affair was in some way connected with the original trouble between her father and Galloway. He was angry with himself for failing to anticipate the attack.

There was a ring at the front-door bell.

"That'll be Trivett," said Tim.

"I've nearly finished," said Dawlish, "and I'm drawing a blank, there's nothing of any use to us here." He turned the unconscious man over and felt in his hip pocket, but it was empty. "No papers, nothing we can identify him by," he said, straightening up, "and Bill will probably say we've taken everything."

The bell was ringing again.

"*Aren't* you going to open the door?" demanded Felicity.

The caller was Trivett. Dawlish ushered him into the small sitting-room.

"Here we are, William," he said, "everything just as you would like it, and the assailant laid out, but not as a corpse."

Trivett looked at the unconscious man grimly.

"You've been laying about him again, have you?"

"A little pressure on his shoulder, that's all," Dawlish assured him; "he fainted at the thought of what might happen to him if you came. I suppose you don't know him, do you?"

Trivett went down on one knee and examined the man.

"No," he said, straightening up. "What did you take from his pockets?"

"Nothing," said Dawlish, blandly. "I looked, but found nothing."

"You're being much too high-handed again," Trivett said. "I

hoped that you would see some sense, now that the Highsea people have shown you that all policemen don't tremble at the name Dawlish. What happened?"

Dawlish told him.

Trivett made no comment and was still considering the suggestion that the man had aimed to kill Muriel, when the door opened to admit Muriel herself, Felicity and the doctor. Rolling was putting on his coat.

"Well?" asked Dawlish, quickly.

"It's not too bad," said Rolling. "The bullet didn't lodge, and it's only just touched the bone. It's a case for the hospital of course. I shall have to telephone for an ambulance. I've given him an injection to put him to sleep for half an hour." He smiled at Trivett. "I see they lost no time in sending for you."

"A pleasant change," said Trivett, shortly.

Rolling went to the telephone and soon began to talk technically to a hospital. Dawlish introduced Muriel, who sat down, and Trivett looked uncertainly at Dawlish, obviously not sure how much to say in front of Muriel.

Dawlish relieved him of any indecision.

"I've been telling the Superintendent, Muriel, that the attack was on you. You'd realized that, hadn't you?"

Muriel exclaimed: "On me? Nonsense!"

She eyed Dawlish with clear hostility. He was surprised at her quick denial, but it seemed to have impressed Trivett. He asked Dawlish why he was so sure, and Dawlish went through his reasoning again. Muriel continued to declare that he was romancing; and Felicity took her part. Tim admitted that he could not feel sure whom the man had intended to attack. Dawlish did not press his point, and Trivett arranged for the man to be taken away. He recovered consciousness before he left, but would not say a word. Before he was gone the ambulance had arrived for Freddie. Muriel declared that she was going to the hospital with him, but at that Rolling put his foot down.

Muriel was almost petulant about it, and gave way with bad grace.

Trivett left a little after nine o'clock. Dawlish sent for dinner for four from the restaurant near by, and the party was glum during the meal. Muriel said practically nothing; Felicity was obviously conscious of the constraint, and did her best to break it. It was Tim who said in desperation:

"We *ought* to go and see Ted."

"Ah, yes," said Dawlish, brightening. "Good idea. Take Felicity, will you, and bless his heart and give him my love."

"Aren't you coming?" demanded Felicity.

"I'll be along," Dawlish assured her. "Muriel and I are going to have a little *tête-à-tête*, aren't we?"

Muriel got up from the table abruptly, and snapped: "No. You seem to be full of nonsensical ideas. *I'm* not going to listen to them." There were tears in her eyes. "I don't know why I went to see you. I don't know . . ."

She turned and hurried into the bedroom. She slammed the door, making Tim stare at it in surprise, and bringing a look of bewilderment to Felicity's eyes. Felicity turned to Dawlish.

"You needn't have upset her, Pat. She's taken it really hard, and—"

"Too hard," said Dawlish. "Muriel has something on her conscience."

"Now, come!" protested Tim.

"There are all the signs of it," Dawlish assured him, "and you'll agree when you think it out for yourself. I wasn't sure until she flew into that tantrum when I suggested that the attack had been made on her. It's not the first sign. She told us of one, if you remember, and said that Galloway's chauffeur was concerned.

Now something has happened not only to frighten her, but to make her feel guilty—"

"Rot!" said Tim, hotly.

Dawlish smiled. "I know it sounds nonsense, but what other explanation is there? She might have been surprised at being selected as the target, she might have been horrified—in fact she could have behaved in a dozen different ways. But it wasn't natural for her simply to utter an indignant denial and then go aloof. You know," he added thoughtfully, "we've never checked on Muriel."

"She did say something about nonsensical ideas," Tim observed, pouring himself out a whisky and soda.

Dawlish laughed. "I've never had an opportunity of a few quiet words with her; she's always avoided that."

"Oh, stop it," said Tim, coming out strongly as Muriel's champion. "Why on earth should she avoid it?"

"It is a fact that she hasn't given me a chance to question her when she's been on her own. By accident or design," Dawlish added, hastily. "But I'm disappointed in you, Tim."

Tim sipped his drink. "What have I been doing wrong?"

"The fellow started to admit that he had come to get Muriel. Why didn't you back me up with her?"

"Because I thought you were backing the wrong horse," Tim told him.

"Oh," said Dawlish, softly. "All pro-Muriel, are we? Don't take me wrong. I like her. There was a quality of merriment in her which I liked. Fel, was there or was there not a quality of merriment about Muriel when she was waiting for us in the bedroom?"

"Yes, of course. She was full of fun."

"Exactly. Do you think Muriel has been full of fun in the last few days, Tim?"

"She's been worried—"

"With nothing more to worry about than she had when she first arrived at the Marine Hotel," Dawlish pointed out; "at least, nothing more that we knew of. Yet, she altered."

"You're *making* trouble!" exploded Tim.

Dawlish sat on the arm of a chair and contemplated him from narrowed eyes. Tim was undoubtedly upset. Dawlish had not previously thought that Tim had been affected. Muriel had contrived to win both these men—Tim quite as much as Freddie, although Tim had shown it less. Neither of them had lost any opportunity to dance attendance on her.

Tim finished his drink. "Look here, Pat, you've made a dead set against Muriel almost from the first."

"All right, have it your own way. I've had a down on the girl. Here are some facts. We've taken Muriel on trust. The police might have checked, although I don't see that they had any reason to—"

"Checked *what?*" demanded Tim.

"Who she is, for a start," said Dawlish. "Oh, yes, I know she had papers with her which seemed to prove her identity. Anyone could have brought those papers of old Lancing's. She might be someone else. She said that her father was dead, after Galloway had said that he was still alive. True, Galloway after-wards confirmed what she said, but we mustn't forget that they might have had a word with each other or Galloway might have managed to get a message of some kind to her. I tell you that soon after Muriel arrived her manner changed remarkably. She certainly wasn't the girl who first saw Felicity and me. They are facts."

Tim looked ill-at-ease. "She hasn't seemed to alter much so far as I've noticed," he said. "It's nonsense to suggest that she might not be who she says she is."

"It might be nonsense to deny that she's Muriel Lancing," said Dawlish, "but it's reasonable enough to say that she *might* be someone else. She's been fairly high in our counsels, too. We'll have to face it out with her, you know. Even you won't be satisfied until she can offer proof of her identity, will you?"

After a prolonged pause, Tim said: "I suppose not. But I don't think there's any doubt."

"Go and see if she'll come in," Felicity urged, and Tim needed no prompting and went quickly to the door.

Tim tapped at the door, but there was no answer. He opened the door, pushed it wider, and then tapped again. "It's Tim," he said. "Muriel, can't you—"

He stopped abruptly, and then pushed the door wider open. The others, alarmed by his manner, hurried forward. He turned and faced them, saying blankly:

"She's gone."

CHAPTER NINETEEN

THE MYSTERY OF MURIEL

It did not take them long to discover how Muriel had escaped from the bedroom. The window led to a small verandah which in turn led to a fire-escape. She had left the window wide open, and it was the strong draught blowing through when Tim opened the door that had made him move so quickly.

Felicity said, "It looks as if you were right, Pat."

"I just can't believe it of *her*," said Tim, helplessly.

"I think there's a mystery about our Muriel," Dawlish said lightly. "We might find out what we can about her—her London address, for instance."

"That's easy," said Tim. "Horton Mews, W.1."

"Not far away," said Dawlish. "Will you go and see whether she's gone home, Tim, and ring me at once if she's there?"

"Yes," said Tim, with a sheepish grin. "Sorry if I was a bit rough, Pat. Er—she's got something, you know."

Dawlish smiled. He hurried to the door with Tim, and saw him down the stairs. Then he returned, and stood for a moment eyeing Felicity speculatively.

"I wonder if she's safe?"

"What do you mean, safe?" asked Felicity. "Do you really think she might let us down?"

"No. I mean that she might be in some danger," said Dawlish. "I don't know whether to wait until we've some news from Tim or whether to get cracking right away. Get cracking, I think." He went to the telephone. Her eyes widened as she exclaimed:

"Not Scotland Yard!"

"We mustn't take chances. I hope Trivett's there."

Trivett soon came on the line.

"Hallo, Pat. What is it now?"

"Bill, I'm worried about Muriel Lancing," Dawlish said. "She left here in a huff a little while after dinner—that's half an hour ago—and I'm not too sure that she's safe. Will you do the necessary?"

Trivett said: "I was thinking only half an hour ago that we didn't know a great deal about her. I was going to ring you. I've got her address somewhere . . ."

"You needn't worry about that," said Dawlish, "but just have a look-out kept for her. I've no special reason, but I'm not sure she's safe."

"What's she been up to?" Trivett asked, suspiciously.

"Having the impudence to be the daughter of Galloway's one-time partner," said Dawlish. "Will you look after her, Bill?"

"You're giving me a proper Sunday out, aren't you?" replied Trivett.

When Dawlish replaced the receiver Felicity was pouring herself a gin and lime. It was not often that she drank, and Dawlish knew that she was greatly upset. He himself was uneasy about Muriel, and even more so about the whole situation.

Felicity put her drink down.

"What are you going to do now?"

"I just don't know," said Dawlish. "I'd like a talk with Galloway or the fair-haired man, or—"

He broke off at the sound of a knock on the front door.

A thump or two on the wood panel, that was all. Dawlish went quickly towards the door. He opened it cautiously.

A man stumbled against the door. Dawlish moved quickly, put an arm about him and helped him into the room.

Felicity exclaimed in a dismayed voice, *"Abbott!"*

Dawlish helped the man to a chair. Only then did he look at him, and he saw the explanation of the dismay in Felicity's voice.

It was Galloway's secretary, and he was badly knocked about. His face was bleeding in several places, there was a nasty cut on his forehead, his lips were puffy and one eye was half-closed. He muttered:

"Gimme—gimme a drink."

"Put on a kettle, will you?" Dawlish said to Felicity. "We'll look after you," he assured the man, and hurried into the bathroom for a towel and some warm water.

It was twenty minutes before he was cleaned up. Not once had he spoken.

"Th-thanks," he said, when he had finished his tea. "Thanks, Dawlish. Could I—could I have a cigarette?"

Dawlish had never like this well-dressed little man, but he had seldom felt more sorry for anyone. Abbott had been beaten up.

Abbott smoked half the cigarette before he spoke again.

"Thanks," he repeated. "You've been very good, Dawlish. I—I had to leave Highsea. I—I had a message from the Old Man."

"From Galloway?"

"Yes. I had to get something from his flat in London, and I went there—"

"Wait a minute," said Dawlish, "the police are watching his flat. Didn't you see them?"

"They're not watching this one," Abbott said. "It's not in his own name, it's a little place he's had on the quiet for years. Calls himself Brown. That's where this happened. I think they thought I was finished, or they wouldn't have gone away."

"Do you know who it was?"

"Yes," said Abbott. "Guy Lancing."

Dawlish looked at him blankly. Felicity, coming from the bathroom, missed a step. Abbott drew in his breath, then said with an effort:

"Didn't you know there was a son? The girl's brother?"

"I didn't," Dawlish said, and reflected bitterly that he had certainly been wrong not to investigate Muriel's story more fully. "Does his sister know he's in England?"

"I expect so," said Abbott. "Don't get me wrong, Dawlish, she's not mixed up with him, she's not like him. There's a streak of the devil in him which *she* hasn't got."

"What's he like?" asked Dawlish, quickly.

"Tall, good-looking, fair-haired," said Abbott, closing his eyes, as if the effort of talking was too much for him. He did not see Dawlish and Felicity exchange glances. "He talks as if butter wouldn't melt in his mouth," Abbott went on, "but he's as bad as they come. He's got two or three roughnecks with him. They're all bad. He was the only man who ever frightened Galloway, until you came along. I can't swear to it, but I think he killed White, it sounded like his men. Sam—Sam's the only one not all bad. You want to be careful of Frazer—Frazer's poison—and the others.

"I don't know all that's happened," he went on, "but I can guess plenty, and one of my guesses is that Guy Lancing was after the *Hedshire* shares, found White was on the same game, bumped him off and then went after the shares White had already bought. We knew White had been buying shares for a long time. Galloway believed he could handle him in the long run, but he wasn't happy about White. White wouldn't use violence, but he was clever. *Too* clever. I think Lancing got him, and I think Lancing gave Galloway that chloroform, to scare him—Lancing wanted to get Galloway good and scared."

What had emerged?

First, Galloway was alive. Second, the fair-haired man was Muriel's brother, son of Galloway's old partner—that could not be emphasized too much, and it might explain what had suddenly affected Muriel. Lancing knew a great deal about Galloway, presumably including his London hiding-place. Lancing and his men had killed White—yes, that was likely. The two dark men whom Beresford had encountered worked for White . . .

No, that was wrong; the two dark men had worked for someone else; Lancing had turned the tables on them.

"Abbott, did Galloway try to get White's *shares?*" asked Dawlish. "Did Galloway employ two little, dark-haired men, one of them named Ken?"

"Sure," said Abbott. "Yes, they were Galloway's men. Galloway was after those shares but couldn't buy them on the open market. And he used those two fellows to do his dirty work. They weren't much good. Galloway's clever in some ways, but he's a fool in others. You never know which way he's going to jump. You can't rely on him from one minute to the next. If you ask me, Galloway's a bit touched."

Dawlish thought that was probably the explanation of the man's extraordinary antics.

"Well, Galloway telephoned me," said Abbott. "I had to clear out of Highsea. I slipped the police; I don't think they know I've left. I went to the flat and ran into Lancing, and you know what happened to me. I came round feeling like hell, and I wanted to break Lancing's neck. I had to do *something*. I don't know where Galloway is, but Lancing says he does. I can't go to the police, so I came to you." His voice rose. "I just can't go on with it, Dawlish, I'm through. I've had to do all that Galloway told me; I'm kicked here and kicked there."

"But why did you let Galloway treat you like that?"

"I didn't have any choice," said Abbott, helplessly. "I just didn't have any choice. Galloway had me where he wanted me; I couldn't break away, but I'm not going back. I'll do my stretch first, I won't go back to Galloway!" His voice rose to a scream.

"Now take it easy. No one's going to send you back to Galloway. Why do you think you'd get a stretch?"

Abbott said: "I used to be a con-man. Galloway knows; he can fix me. I just don't know what to do, Dawlish. I've worked for Galloway for four years; it gets worse, it—"

"Do you say you don't know where he is?"

"I'd tell you if I did!"

"I'm sure you would," said Dawlish, soothingly. "Do you know where he might be?"

"I haven't the faintest," said Abbott. "There's only two places: his flat in Park Lane and the little place in Chelsea where I've just come from. They're the only places I know about."

"Good enough," said Dawlish. "But why did he want to get *Hedshire Estates* shares? What's their value?"

Abbott said in a tense voice: "I don't know that, either. He wouldn't trust me. He had some papers in that brief-case I told you about; I think the secret was in there. White didn't know, either. All White knew was that Galloway wanted them back, and he started after them in competition. Galloway wanted them badly. White would have sold them back to him, at a price.

That was White's game. He told you the truth, I think: he was sold on *Hedshire's* and got a lot of people to buy; that was true. It wasn't until he learned that Galloway was after them again that he realized there was any salvage, so he took a chance."

"Does Lancing know why Galloway wants them back?"

"He might," said Abbott, "but I don't think he does. He asked me where Galloway was at first; he made me think that was what he wanted, and then he started on asking me why Galloway wanted the shares. It was terrible. He put Frazer on to me. He started with Sam, but Sam's not so bad, there's limits to what Sam will do, but then he put Frazer on to me. I passed out three times," he added, gasping. "I thought they were never going to let up. And then I come round and they was gone. I think they thought they'd done for me." He was trembling from head to foot.

"Pat," said Felicity, in a small voice, "he ought to have some rest."

"Yes," agreed Dawlish. "We'd better make up the small-room bed."

"I've seen to it," said Felicity.

"Come on, Abbott, you want some rest." Abbott tried to get up, but could not make it. Dawlish lifted him effortlessly and carried him into the bedroom. He took off his shoes and his coat.

He left the darkened room, closed the door quietly, and lit a cigarette.

"It isn't often you get anything on a plate," said Felicity, after a pause. "You must have made a favourable impression on him."

Dawlish grinned. "This has helped a lot. The main query now is why Galloway wants *Hedshire Estates* stock back, but I suppose we'll find that out eventually. One thing's certain," he added, "it's not exactly waste-paper. Good tidings for all the owners of the stock."

"Including the Dawlish family," said Felicity, brightening. "Pat—I suppose Muriel knew about her brother?"

"Yes," said Dawlish. "That's the betting. I wish I knew more about that family."

"I wish we knew where Muriel was," said Felicity. "I wonder who tried to kill her? Was it one of Galloway's men or one of Lancing's?"

Dawlish started. "My sweet, you've got it!"

"Got it?" asked Felicity, mystified.

"The reason for Muriel's urgent denial!" cried Dawlish. "She thought that the gunman came from her brother, and she wouldn't admit that he had sent someone to kill her. If that gunman did come from Lancing, do you know what it means?"

"What?"

"Lancing thinks his sister can give the whole game away," reasoned Dawlish, "and as Lancing apparently didn't know why Galloway wanted the shares but *did* know where Galloway is hiding, he presumably thinks Muriel knows that too. He wanted to stop Muriel from telling us where he might be."

"We haven't heard from Tim," said Felicity.

She had hardly finished speaking before the telephone rang. It was Tim, troubled and grave-voiced.

"Any luck?" asked Dawlish, quickly.

"Not yet," said Tim. "But one or two odd things have turned up, Pat. I've been to Muriel's flat. She did call in there. She shares it with another girl, a rather chatty piece. A *very* odd thing happened. Muriel was only there for ten minutes, but just after she'd gone someone turned up and inquired for her. This chatty piece says that the man told her he is Muriel's brother."

"And he's got fair hair," said Dawlish.

Tim exclaimed, "Are you on to that already?"

"Yes, but you did the detective work, mine came on a plate," said Dawlish. "And we know now that Muriel was aware of the existence of her brother. Odd that she didn't confide, isn't it?"

"It's all odd," said Tim, gruffly. "I missed this fellow, Guy Lancing, by about ten minutes. The chatty piece gave me an address—but it's an old one, in a block of flats. But I *think* I can find out his new address from it. His letters are re-addressed from the flats. The porter's off duty, but I've found out where he lives. Shall I go after him?"

"We'll go after him," said Dawlish, eagerly. "A word with Guy Lancing would do a world of good. Where are you?"

"In the porter's office, with the night-duty man. He's a new chum, and doesn't know Lancing's forwarding address."

"Where does the other porter live?"

"In Fulham—17 Eelbrook Road," said Tim, "not far from Wandsworth Bridge Road. Shall I meet you there?"

"Yes," said Dawlish. "In half an hour. Nice work, Tim."

A ring at the front door heralded Ted Beresford, a Ted in a daze of delight, who beamed about him and drank beer absently, and seemed to find it difficult to concentrate on anything but his offspring. He would be delighted, he said, to keep Felicity company for an hour or two. And if anyone did come along and threaten trouble he, Ted, was in just the right mood for them. Oh, there was one thing Dawlish ought to know. Just before he had left the nursing-home, a policeman johnny had arrived. Very affable and all that, but rather anxious to know whether he was going straight back home after seeing his wife, or whether he was doing anything for Dawlish.

Beresford grinned. "He thought I was in a mood where I would fall for anything," he said, "but I told him a story of much mystery, and I expect he's telling Trivett quite a tale. Are you working with Trivett?"

"Up to a point," said Dawlish.

"Oughtn't you to stretch the point?" asked Felicity.

Dawlish said: "I don't think so, until we've been able to find out what Muriel does know. With Tim and Freddie smitten as they are, we want to know the worst before the police. Reasonable?" he asked.

"What difference will it make?" asked Felicity.

"I don't quite know," said Dawlish, "but I think we'd better try to find this part out for ourselves. We've got the police on the look-out, so she shouldn't come to any harm. She may have gone to see her brother, of course, and if she has—"

He broke off, and shrugged his shoulders. Then he went into the main bedroom and took out two service revolvers, with ammunition.

Dawlish hurried downstairs. Exactly half an hour after he had spoken to Tim he reached 17 Eelbrook Road.

Tim was waiting beneath a street lamp.

"Have you seen the porter?" asked Dawlish.

"Yes. Lancing's address cost a fiver," said Tim.

"It was worth it. Where does he live?"

"Fortescue Court, Bayswater," Tim told him, "and Fortescue Court is in a side street off the Bayswater Road. A large house, divided into flats." They got into a cab, which drove off.

Dawlish told Tim what he had learned from Abbott. They reached Fortescue Court as he finished, and soon were standing outside the first-floor flat, which had the name Larking—*not* Lancing—on the door.

There was a light inside.

CHAPTER TWENTY

BROTHER AND SISTER

The landing was in darkness, and the house was quiet. Dawlish and Tim stood for some seconds.

Dawlish took out his torch. Tim shone the light on the lock, and Dawlish took out a penknife. It was not long before the lock clicked back.

There was a light in the hall, and they could hear voices, coming from a room on the left. But there was a light under another door.

Dawlish pointed to it.

A woman's voice alternated with a man's. They could not be sure that it was Muriel's. The second door was unlocked. Dawlish opened the door a few inches. Smoke floated out; the room was hazy and yet bright. Dawlish prepared for an alarm, but there was no other sound except a gruff voice saying:

"Your deal."

Dawlish opened the door a little further, and saw three men sitting about a card-table. One had his back to the door, the others were sideways towards it, and all of them were concentrating on the dealer. That was Frazer. 'Sam' the thug had his back towards Dawlish, and the third man was he who had brought the alarm to Lancing and his men at Hollway Mansions.

Dawlish took out his gun, and Tim joined him. They went forward, and had gone half-way towards the table before Frazer noticed them. He sat quite still, with two cards left in his hand for dealing.

Dawlish said, "I don't think we'll have any noise."

Sam turned round like a well-sprung toy, but did not speak. The third man uttered a low-pitched gasp. Three pairs of eyes were turned towards Dawlish, who spoke again in a low-pitched voice:

"Stand up, and face the window."

None of them moved and none of them spoke.

"I mean it," Dawlish said.

Frazer said thinly, "Who the hell do you think you are?"

"Friends of Beresford," Dawlish said.

Sam said, "Strewth, it's Dawlish, and he's *bigger'n* Beresford!"

"And also packs a punch," said Dawlish. "Don't make me use it; I've taken a liking to you, Sam."

Frazer was sliding his hand towards his pocket. "You can't get away with anything. I've only got to raise my voice—"

"To get badly hurt," Dawlish said. "Put your hands up!" He thrust the gun forward, and Frazer snatched his hand away and thrust it towards the ceiling. "Sam, you're an expert, I think, but watch this."

Tim had been edging towards the men. He stretched out his hand, holding a gun by the barrel.

Tim said, as the last fell: "It's easier than I expected, Pat. How are they doing next door?"

There had been surprisingly little noise. Dawlish turned and went into the hall. The man was still talking. There was nothing to suggest that he knew what was happening outside.

Dawlish locked the door on Frazer and his companions.

Suddenly they heard Muriel's voice.

"I tell you no!"

"There's no need to get heated, Sis," said Lancing, and then his voice dropped.

Dawlish opened the door an inch. They heard the tail-end of what he was saying.

"I don't want to make trouble for you. I want everything to go off nice and quietly, but you're being too difficult."

"I won't have anything to do with it," Muriel said, tensely.

"You mustn't be obstinate. After all, it *is* our money, Sis. Galloway made the old man go broke. He ruined him; we're only getting our own back."

"Not this way," said Muriel.

"It's the only way we can," said Lancing.

"If you hadn't been such a swine—"

"Now, Sis," said Lancing, sharply, "I've told you before, I don't want to hurt you. If you'll play ball with me, you will come well out of this. I don't think your share will be much under a hundred thousand pounds. All you've got to do is to tell me where I can find Galloway. Then you can go home. There needn't be anything on your conscience."

Muriel said bitterly, "I know what you've been doing."

"Just forget it," said Lancing.

"And I suppose I've got to forget that you sent a man to shoot me," she said. "Dawlish was right."

"Never mind Dawlish," said Lancing. "I'm glad that I've discovered the truth about you, Sis. I thought you were such a good girl, but you wouldn't mind helping me if it weren't for the fear of being hurt. You needn't worry. You were dangerous when you were with Dawlish but you're not dangerous now. All you've got to do is to tell me where to find Galloway. After that you'll be as free as the air. What could be fairer than that?"

Lancing's voice sharpened. "I'm not going to waste any more time. You've been here for nearly an hour, and you're as stubborn now as when you came in. Do you want me to make Frazer work on you?"

Muriel caught her breath.

"Or haven't you heard of Frazer?" asked Lancing, with a sneer. "You should have seen Abbott after he'd finished with him. He never lets sentiment interfere with business. He handled White, too. And the man who looked like Galloway. I actually had Galloway here, but he was clever enough to get away. I hoped the police would think he'd done a flit and left the corpse as a stooge. Probably they'll blame Galloway for it yet. But you haven't met Frazer yet, have you? He has one or two bright ideas with the fair sex. They ought to be effective. Let's stop fooling. Where's Galloway?"

Muriel said, "Have you *completely* forgotten I'm your sister?"

"If you weren't, I wouldn't waste this time on you," said Lancing. "But don't run away with the idea that it will help you if you don't play. What do you mean to me?" There was a sharp sound, as if he had snapped his fingers. "That much! I haven't seen you for fifteen years. You'd almost forgotten that I ever existed. And there are one or two other things you've forgotten. I've spent half my life in jail, and the other half being broke. It's only since I discovered what Galloway was after that I came into the money, and I'm *staying* in the money." He paused. "*Why does Galloway want the shares back?*"

There was no answer.

"Come on," said Lancing, with a savage note in his voice. "I want to know the other thing, too. What does Galloway know about the land? Why's he after the shares?"

A chair scraped. Dawlish and Tim grew tense.

Muriel said in a low-pitched voice, "If I knew where to find

Galloway I wouldn't tell you, and if I knew why he wanted the shares I wouldn't tell you that."

Lancing said thickly, "You wait until you've met Frazer."

"Never mind Frazer," said Muriel. There was a heavy sound, as of footsteps; Lancing was coming towards the door. *"Stop where you are!"* cried Muriel, and there was a different note in her voice; she seemed to have gained confidence.

Lancing began, "Shut up, you—" and then broke off. There was an appreciable pause before he roared, "Put that gun away!"

Outside the door, Dawlish and Tim exchanged glances.

"Stay there," ordered Muriel, and the tone of her voice seemed to make Lancing stop.

Dawlish wished that he dare open the door farther, but thought it wiser not to.

Inside the room, Lancing was standing two yards in front of his sister. The small gun in her hand was quite steady. Her hair was dishevelled, where he had pulled it only a moment before, but her eyes were calm. The big room seemed very still.

"Put—that—away," he said, heavily.

"I've got something to say to you," said Muriel, in a steady voice. "You can listen now. For years I've thought about you, wondered what you were doing, wondered what kind of man you had turned out to be. I knew nothing about you after you'd left home. You hurt Mother more than you'll ever realize, but the years made me forget that. I cared for you."

"Cut this slush out," growled Lancing. "It's—"

"Listen to me! I heard nothing about you until Father came home last year. He told me where you'd been, what you'd been doing. He told me that he thought Galloway had turned you bad. He told me that he thought there was good in you, and he begged me to try to help you. I've wanted to find you ever since, but didn't know where to look. I didn't know you were in England, until Galloway told me."

"Galloway!" ejaculated Lancing.

"Yes, he knew," said Muriel. "I went down to Highsea to see Dawlish. I hated Galloway as much as you did. I wanted to find out the truth about him; I wanted to help Dawlish or the police to catch him—and then he telephoned me, the first night I was at the hotel. He told me that you were working against him. He'd actually told Dawlish that it was Father, but it was you. He knew, you see, what a sentimental fool I had been over you. When I lived at his house I talked about you a great deal. He told me to try to get Dawlish to go away, and he warned me that if I didn't I would learn unpleasant things about you. He told me that you had been responsible for the murder of White. He almost convinced me that there might be something in it, but I wasn't satisfied. I did—nothing. I wanted to see you.

"When I came back here I intended to try to find you. When I realized that someone had fired to try to kill me, I hated the thought that you might be responsible. But I still gave you a chance. I went to my flat and I got this gun—I've had it for a long time. I knew where you lived, because Galloway told me. So I came here to see you; I hoped that I would learn that Galloway was wrong. I learned the ugly truth about you. I don't know how many men you've got here, I don't know what might happen if I let you go. I'm not going to let you go. I'm going to shoot you, as you tried to shoot me."

Lancing drew in his breath. "Sis, be sensible, be—"

"I'm quite sensible," Muriel said. "When I've shot you I'm going to see Dawlish and I'm going to tell him everything I know about you, everything I know about Galloway, everything that has happened. I don't greatly care what happens to me now.

All I care about is finishing a job which should have been done years ago."

"Don't be a fool, Sis! If you fire, Frazer and the others will come rushing in; they're armed, you won't have a chance. And when Frazer has finished with you, you'll be—" He broke off.

"I'll risk that," said Muriel, and there was no doubt that she meant it.

Dawlish opened the door and stepped inside.

Muriel saw him first and backed away in alarm and astonishment. Lancing moved before Dawlish or Tim could act. He knocked the gun out of her grasp, and then he seized her throat between his hands. He squeezed.

Muriel drew in one terrible breath and then choked . . .

Dawlish struck Lancing's head with the butt of his gun. A savage blow, and Lancing crumpled up. His hands relaxed and Muriel dropped into a chair. Dawlish pushed Lancing out of his way, picked the girl up, and made sure that she was getting her breath back.

Tim snapped, "How is she?"

"She'll be all right," said Dawlish. "We needn't worry. You and Freddie needn't worry, either. It's as well we came along, there might have been some misunderstanding if the police had found her first. I'll make sure they're all right in the next room. We've been here a long time."

Only Sam, of the three men in the next room, was conscious. Dawlish spent five minutes tying their legs and arms to make sure that they could not attempt to get away, and then went back into the other room.

Muriel was sitting up, looking better, although her neck was swollen and red. She was sipping a glass of water, and Tim was holding her free hand. When she caught sight of Dawlish she put the glass down.

"Just bad, right through, my father and my brother. I can't get over *that*."

"For such a big girl you say a lot of silly things," said Dawlish, lightly. "You *are* over it."

"Tainted with—"

"Get some sense into your noddle," said Dawlish, with feeling. "Don't go about with foolish ideas of being tainted with bad blood. You've done all you can *to* see it through, and you didn't do so badly."

"It isn't as easy as that," she said.

Dawlish smiled. "Felicity and Freddie between them will shake that nonsense out of you," he declared, "and it *is* nonsense. But you can still make a job of it," he went on, "you can tell us what Galloway wants the shares for."

She said in a low-pitched voice, "No, I can't."

Dawlish frowned. "But your brother thought—"

"My brother thought I knew and thought I was working with Galloway," she said. "I haven't any idea what Galloway is doing and I don't know where he is. That's true—Pat, it's true."

"It's obviously true, but it's still a disappointment. All you've had to do with Galloway was the single telephone conversation, wasn't it?"

"Yes. Yes, but—"

"Well?" asked Dawlish, encouragingly.

"He must have some reason," Muriel said, weakly. She sat there looking at him desperately. "If we could repay those people who lost so much on *Hedshire Estates* I'd feel much better."

"Well, that shouldn't be so hard," Dawlish said. "The shares are valuable because the so-called waste-land must have some value we know nothing about. Galloway knows. Galloway has some of the shares, your brother has others here, and all can be returned to the original owners. There are some people who still have their shares, and when the true value comes on the market, everything in the garden will be lovely."

"But you haven't got Galloway!"

"Well, he's about, and there's reasonable evidence that he's alive," Dawlish said. "The police will get him, eventually."

"I'm not so sure," said Muriel.

"Why not?"

"You see, I know him," she said, in a tense voice. "He's always had one care above all others—his own fat body, his comfort and his safety. I don't think he'll stay in England. I don't think he'll realize on the *Hedshires*. He'll just go away, and—"

"But he won't be allowed to go away," objected Dawlish.

"Can you be sure of stopping him?"

"Pretty sure," said Dawlish. "I wouldn't like to be Galloway trying to get out of the country with the police in their present mood."

"He can fly out of the country, can't he?"

"It isn't as easy as you think," Dawlish said.

"You just don't know Galloway!" She stood up, trembling. "I can't bear it if he gets away; *everything* depends on it—"

The telephone bell interrupted her.

Dawlish looked round the room and saw the instrument in a corner.

A man spoke. "I want to speak to Mr. *Larking*, please."

Dawlish recognized the voice.

Galloway was at the other end of the line.

CHAPTER TWENTY-ONE

CHASE

There would never be another opportunity like this.

Dawlish made a quick sign to Tim. "Have the call traced," he whispered. "Hallo," said Dawlish. He was trying to recall Lancing's voice well enough to imitate it. It was worth trying. In any case the call would soon be traced.

Tim was already out of the room.

Dawlish tried his luck. "Larking speaking," he said. "Who is that?"

"I'm not going to tell you my name," said Galloway, "but I knew your father very well, Mr. *Lancing*." That dig was characteristic of Galloway. "I was a close friend of your father's, and your sister was my guest for some time."

Dawlish gasped, "Gallo—"

"Hush!" breathed Galloway. "Don't say anything silly now. It concerns some shares—you—er—you bought a number of them today, I believe. I heard it rumoured; you see, I have my spies."

"I know what you mean," said Dawlish.

"I'm sure you do. What you *don't* know is what the shares

are worth and why they are so valuable," said Galloway. "Now that is important, my boy, and my proposition concerns those important things. I want to talk to you—tonight."

"I can't—" began Dawlish.

"You can and will meet me tonight. Or *very* early in the morning—dear me, it is after eleven o'clock. It will have to be about one o'clock. Come to Putney Bridge, the Putney side of the bridge, where a closed car will be waiting for you."

Dawlish said, "I don't have to come."

"Oh, don't you?" asked Galloway, softly. "Do you want the police to know where you are, and that Larking and Lancing are one and the same? Do you want them to know that you authorized the shooting of a policeman at Chiswick? That you had White killed, you had that unfortunate man who looked like me killed—and you had *me* chloroformed."

"Damn you!" snapped Dawlish, and hoped he sounded vicious enough. There was little to worry about now, that call would be traced.

"Don't be so small-minded," Galloway rebuked him. "I think perhaps you had better have someone with you, though. You will be happier, I expect. Not Frazer, I dislike that man very much. Sam—yes, perhaps Sam." He paused. "Are you so surprised that you do not ask *how* it is I know your staff so well?"

Dawlish said, "You said you had your spies."

"And I have," chuckled Galloway; "you will be watched. At one o'clock, sharp, on the Putney side of Putney Bridge. The car will be a Wolseley 14. Now I must go. Be careful, Lancing, and if the police *are* listening in to your telephone conversations and they prevent you from reaching here, don't be foolish enough to tell them too much, will you?"

He rang off.

His last words jolted Dawlish out of his high spirits; Galloway knew the possibility that the call would be traced, and was in no wise disturbed. That wasn't so good. Tim came in, nodding with satisfaction. "How did things go, Tim?"

Tim put a thumb up.

"As smoothly as that," he said. "Trivett was still at the office, and he doesn't lose much time. He said he was coming here himself."

Very soon after, Trivett arrived with Inspector Davy. They stared when they saw Lancing on the floor, and Muriel's state of dishevelment.

"Well, where's Galloway?" asked Dawlish.

Trivett said heavily, "I don't know. I've just heard the news over the radio. The call came from Highbury, a call-box near the junction of several roads; awkward, even at this time of night. Our men got there, they actually saw Galloway, but he managed to get away. They're looking for him."

"Well, that leaves only one reasonable hope."

"Which one?" demanded Trivett.

"He made an appointment on the Putney side of Putney Bridge," said Dawlish. "With Lancing, not me, but perhaps I'll do."

"Now, let me know everything," Trivett insisted.

Dawlish told him while Davy and Tim were untying the men in the other room. The picture gradually formed in Trivett's mind, and when it was over he had the grace to admit that Dawlish had done the obviously wise thing. Dawlish remarked casually that it was getting on for midnight, so they had to decide what to do about the appointment with Galloway.

"*I'll* keep that," said Trivett.

"I hope you won't," said Dawlish, promptly. "You'll come to a sticky end if you go there instead of Lancing."

"And what about you?" asked Trivett.

Dawlish said: "If I go, that will probably tickle Galloway's sense of humour. And if I take Sam with me, it will do even more. There isn't any reason why you shouldn't have the bridge watched. You can have cars waiting near all the main roads, without lights."

"I'm afraid you're right," Trivett said, slowly.

The only real argument developed about whether Sam should go with Dawlish. Dawlish wanted him, Trivett was against it. Dawlish did not force the issue, but when, at the last moment, Trivett agreed, he was delighted.

Dawlish used Ted Beresford's car.

One police-car followed him, and Trivett had already arranged for the police to be watching the bridge. There was little chance that Galloway would get away if he came here, but Dawlish doubted very much whether he would come in person.

They were turning into Fulham Palace Road and towards the bridge, when Sam broke his self-imposed silence.

"Want to know something? The Boss doesn't like you," said Sam. "Much."

"Well, he can't do any harm now," said Dawlish.

"Oh, I don't mean Lancing," said Sam, scornfully.

"Whom do you mean?"

"Why, Galloway," said Sam, calmly. "He's the Boss. I been working for him a long time. Does it surprise you, Guv'nor?"

Dawlish said heavily, "Very much indeed." He wished as he had rarely wished for anything that he had not brought Sam with him, that for once Trivett had refused to be persuaded. The calmness of the man by his side was unnerving.

"Yes," said Dawlish, slowing down, "it surprises me a lot. I think I'd better drop you, Sam."

"What, *me*?" Sam looked at him in pained surprise. "You don't want to do that," he protested. "I'm through with Galloway. You needn't worry about having me along. There's the car," he added, as they stopped at the side of the bridge. On the other side was a Wolseley 14, with its side and rear lights on. "That's Galloway's," he said, and then Dawlish felt a restraining hand on his arm. "Don't get out yet," pleaded Sam.

"I arranged—"

"Sure, I've been told what you arranged, but don't get out yet," said Sam. "I know Galloway. He doesn't like you much. He didn't like Lancing at all. You think he is going to do a deal with Lancing, don't you?"

Dawlish felt his flesh going cold. "What do you mean?"

"Just supposing," said Sam, "I'm Lancing. I get out. I walked across the road to the Wolseley. I'm halfway there, and something happens. I stop halfway, and I don't get up. Don't you kid yourself," Sam said, sombrely, "that's what would happen supposing I was Lancing. But I'm not—I'm Sam, and Sam's reliable. I get out. I say to the chauffeur, Lancing won't play your way. Lancing gonner drive after us. And I say it doesn't matter where he gets Lancing, better out on the common or out in the country. So we drive off and you follow. That's the play."

"I see," said Dawlish, slowly. He was conscious of the lurking police. He felt cold at the thought of what might have happened had he followed his own inclinations.

Then he told himself that he was placing too much reliance on Sam. What Sam probably wanted was an opportunity to escape. Dawlish hesitated, and Sam opened the door.

"Okay?" he asked.

'Well, he won't get away,' thought Dawlish. 'It's worth risking.' "All right," he said aloud, and Sam opened the door and stepped into the road.

There were three shots from the gun in the Wolseley driver's hand, a shudder through Sam's body before he fell, followed by the roar of the engine as it started off. Police appeared from hiding-places on the bridge, three cars started off immediately, but the Wolseley made a quick turn by the island near the bridge, and roared off up Putney High Street. The noise of the engine was so great that Dawlish realized that it was supercharged.

One police-car swung across the road in front of Dawlish, skidded, and crashed into a lamp-standard. Dawlish swung the wheel, missed the other car by inches, and started off along the High Street. Two other police-cars were in front of him, but the Wolseley had stolen a march on all the drivers, and was at least a hundred yards ahead, making for the open road across Wimbledon Common.

Dawlish passed the first police-car. The other was going fast now, and Dawlish settled down to third place.

Once up the hill, Dawlish opened the throttle. Soon he was level with the police-car. He saw Trivett waving him on. Then he was past, the Wolseley in front of him.

The red light of the Wolseley was perhaps two hundred yards away. They were driving along the Kingston by-pass. The man would have to slow down soon at one of the roundabouts. Dawlish thought that he might gain a little then.

He saw the Wolseley swerve. Next moment the red light disappeared. Did that mean that it had rounded the roundabout and gone straight on, or had it turned right or left? In a sweat of anxiety he watched the road. There was no roundabout, only cross-roads, so the car had turned right or left. He had no idea which. He had seen no lights . . .

A car was travelling towards him, and in the glow of its head-lights he saw another car, *the Wolseley*, travelling without lights. Just a trick. The Wolseley was much nearer now, and it was travelling much more slowly. Suddenly its lights went on again. Dawlish grinned to himself as he overtook it. Why had the man suddenly given up the race? Was this a trick, intended to take him unawares? Was shooting about to start again?

He passed the Wolseley, then swung in front of it and put on his brakes. The bumpers of the Wolseley touched the rear bumpers of his car. A querulous voice demanded:

"What the devil do you think *you're* doing?"

Dawlish was out of the car in a flash. The bowler-hatted man was leaning out of the window of the Wolseley, pouring out a tirade of abuse, yet he looked a frightened and timid little man. Then he saw Dawlish's gun, and his words stopped.

"Get out!" snapped Dawlish, and the man opened the door and stepped out, backing away from the gun. There seemed no one else in the car. Keeping the driver covered, Dawlish opened the back door and looked in to make sure.

The driver said, "I—I'll have the police on you!"

"You'll have the police on you for driving without lights. Turn round," said Dawlish, so sharply that the man obeyed without hesitation. He did not carry a gun.

The headlights of another car appeared, and the little man in front of Dawlish muttered:

"I—I've got to get home. I haven't got anything worth taking, leave me alone, and—"

"Just keep quiet," Dawlish said, and then the other car pulled up, and Trivett jumped out. With him was a uniformed constable, and at the sight of the uniform the Wolseley's driver broke into a torrent of accusation.

"Just a moment, please. Dawlish, what's happened?"

Carefully, and with increasing bitterness, Dawlish explained. Trivett, completely taken aback, looked at the Wolseley driver accusingly, and began to ask questions. Then, almost ingratiatingly, the man told his story—a very simple and straightforward one. He was a commercial traveller who lived at Guildford; he had been to an association dinner in London and decided that he would try to get home for the night. Near Putney he had developed tyre trouble, and it had taken him some time to change the wheel. Then his lights had failed him. Sometimes they worked and sometimes they went off. He had only a few miles to go. His name? Yes, of course he would give his name and address, and everyone in the firm of Arnoldsen & Co., of Billitter Street, would vouch for him. They could ring his wife up, if they liked.

"Well," said Trivett, "it looks as if we've had it."

"You've put a call out for a Wolseley, I hope?" said Dawlish.

"Yes, but it's a bad time for stopping everything on the road."

"Are you going to ring my wife, or aren't you?"

"There's an A.A. box just along the road, sir."

"Go and telephone this gentleman's house, please," said Trivett. The fact that he left that task to his man told Dawlish how much he had taken this business to heart. The futility of it all had come home to Dawlish. The simplicity of the manœuvre, and the blind luck which the Wolseley driver had met, turning off the main road with another Wolseley only a few yards in front of him . . . Blind luck! Was it?

"We may as well search the car, I suppose," Trivett said.

"Yes," agreed Dawlish. There was a thought at the back of his mind which grew more insistent. *Could* the timid little man be bluffing? He opened the car door again and sniffed, in the hope that there would be a smell of cordite. There was not. He lifted the back seats, but found only a few tools.

"Nothing here," said Trivett.

Dawlish sighed. "I didn't see a car turn right or left at those crossroads. Assume that no car turned off the road, but our commercial is pulling a fast one. Supposing he knew he couldn't get away, and slowed down, switched off his lights, and bluffed?

What would be the strength of his hand? He would know that the police would take the usual precautions, so he wouldn't lie about his home, where he's been tonight, and the mood of his wife. All those things would be sound enough, but none of them prevent him from being the man who shot Sam."

Trivett said slowly, "No, I suppose not."

"Galloway could have given him his instructions by telephone, after he had left this dinner," Dawlish said. "He's explained any lapse of time between the close of the dinner and his arrival here by delays due to tyre trouble. That can't easily be proved one way or the other. He could have thrown the gun out of the window, after wiping his prints off it, and kept the windows open to clear out any smell. I think we ought to follow him home. He mustn't know, of course; he must be lulled into thinking that he's got away with it. Supposing we follow him, and supposing he immediately telephones Galloway with the latest news? We'd have something if we were close on his heels. We'd have to take a chance or two, of course. But it may be our last."

"I don't think there's a chance of learning anything," Trivett said, "but I'll take you."

"Good man!" exclaimed Dawlish, and added eagerly: "You might get Oates to telephone the Guildford Exchange and get all calls from this fellow's number checked over."

Oates came back with the commercial traveller and a report that the man's wife had verified all his statements and the number of his car. The Wolseley driver, whose name was Hammley, asked testily whether he was to be allowed to go.

"In a few minutes," said Trivett. "Oates . . ."

He gave the man whispered instructions, and then he and Dawlish set off in the Lagonda, starting towards London. At the first crossroads Dawlish turned. Soon they were driving past Oates, who was getting out of Trivett's car outside the A.A. box.

Hammley was some way off, driving at good speed, apparently having no difficulty with his lights.

Dawlish said, "We'll pass him and wait farther along."

"All right," said Trivett.

Half an hour later they saw Hammley turn into a wide, tree-lined avenue on the outskirts of Guildford.

They left the car at the end of the road and hurried along, reaching the house in time to see Hammley closing the front door. The car, apparently, had been put in a garage.

"Now if you really want to get results, you'll turn your back on me for a few minutes," said Dawlish. "But if you should afterwards decide to wait in the porch in case someone gets thrown out on his ear—"

Trivett said gruffly, "I'm going to have a look round the back; you watch the front, will you?"

He walked past an open window . . .

Two minutes later Dawlish was inside the house. He could hear a couple talking. The man kept laughing; the woman's voice held a note of admiration. Dawlish listened intently.

"No, it wasn't Lancing," said Hammley, "I think it was Sam, and he got what was coming to him. I think the big customer who caught me up was Dawlish. And that Superintendent, Trivett—it was the easiest job I've ever handled."

"You've done marvels, Dave," said the woman. "I'm just a little worried because the old man's still here; he ought to go soon, didn't he? The police might come and ask questions, and they might want to look round."

Hammley laughed. "How's the old man been?"

"He stayed up until half past twelve, and then said he'd better have some rest. I went and told him the police had been through, and he laughed and said he wouldn't worry about getting up, as it was all right. He's got some nerve, Dave."

"His money's good. We can keep him tucked away for a bit; the police will never find out where we've got him." He laughed smugly. "I'd better go and report."

The couple went along the passage by the stairs. Dawlish waited until they had disappeared, leaving the door ajar, and then followed swiftly.

Dawlish watched Hammley standing in the kitchen, with his wife by his side. For Hammley was taking away a part of the kitchen range. Then he inserted a key into a small hole in the wall. He pushed, and a narrow door opened.

'So he was safe enough,' Dawlish thought, remembered Trivett standing on the porch, and stepped forward, gun in hand. He whispered: "My turn, I think."

Hammley made a dive for the passage beyond, but Dawlish was near enough to grab him. He pulled him back, and said to his wife, "Go to the front door, Mrs. Hammley."

Dazedly, she obeyed him. Dawlish pushed Hammley along in front of him. It was Mrs. Hammley who opened the door to a startled Trivett, who was backing away in surprise.

Hammley and his wife did not utter a word. Trivett slipped the handcuffs on.

The passage was hardly large enough for Dawlish to pass along with comfort, but it was short, and led to a flight of steps. At the foot of the steps was a closed door.

It was unlocked, and they stepped through into a small, well-furnished sitting-room, with two doors leading off it.

The first door led to a bathroom; the second to a bedroom, where, on a double bed, Galloway was fast asleep.

Dawlish grinned. "Fair cop," he said, and stepped forward.

Galloway woke with a start. He blinked, and hitched himself up on his pillows. He put one hand outside the bedclothes, and began to push them back, but he kept the other hand under cover.

"Come—*on!*" exhorted Dawlish, and flung the clothes back.

Galloway's right hand was clutching a small automatic. Trivett snatched at it. Galloway got his hands free, and fired. His bullet passed between Dawlish and the Superintendent, and hit the ceiling. Next moment Trivett had the gun in his hand, and Dawlish hauled Galloway out of bed. He stood trembling in pale-blue silk pyjamas, looking plump and absurd.

Trivett said: "Immanuel Galloway, I arrest you in connection with the murder of Samuel Godders, and I must warn you that anything you say may be used in evidence. Get dressed quickly."

When he was ready to go, Dawlish said, "Just one thing, Galloway. Why were you so anxious to get *Hedshire Estates* shares back? You were after them, weren't you?"

Galloway cried, "Of course—of course! *That* wasn't criminal, that was a matter of business. After—after I had sold the land to *Hedshire Estates*—and what fools they were to buy, what fools they were!—I made a remarkable discovery. Deep down, much deeper down than it is usually found, were *rich* deposits of iron ore, Dawlish. *Rich* deposits. And think! Iron ore, so near to such a thriving industrial city as Birmingham—what a fortune can be made out if it! I intended to make quite sure that the development of the land was not only to my advantage, but to the advantage of the people who had invested in the land already. Aren't you glad, Dawlish?"

Dawlish said, "I'm delighted!"

"There," beamed Galloway. "There, you see, Mr. Dawlish is pleased. Everyone will be pleased. And when this foolish misunderstanding has been dealt with—"

"And you really think you might get away with that," marvelled Dawlish.

"Come along," said Trivett, gruffly.

*   *   *

There was little disclosed at the trials of Lancing and Galloway that was new to Dawlish. The story as it had gradually built itself up was finally established. White's part, buying the shares because he knew Galloway was on a good thing; Lancing's part with a similar motive but the additional one that he had nursed a grudge against Galloway for most of his life; Galloway's part, mostly the financial side—all these things were proved.

Sam had died.

Galloway and the Hammleys were convicted of his murder. Lancing and Frazer were convicted of the murder of White and Galloway's stooge. And White, it was proved, had tried to poison Galloway.

Galloway admitted paying Dawlish £25,000 to quieten him; his life would have been cheap at the price.

A Government Commission was appointed to investigate the truth about *Hedshire Estates* property. Galloway had been right, there were great commercial prospects for the land. All over the country people who had considered their shares as little pieces of waste paper were coming to realize the truth.

Every share which had been bought by White or obtained by Galloway and Lancing was resold to its original owner.

ABOUT THE AUTHOR

John Creasey, born in 1908, was a paramount English crime and science fiction writer who used myriad pseudonyms for more than six hundred novels. He founded the UK Crime Writers' Association in 1953. In 1962, his book *Gideon's Fire* received the Edgar Award for Best Novel from the Mystery Writers of America. Many of the characters featured in Creasey's titles became popular, including George Gideon of Scotland Yard, who was the basis for a subsequent television series and film. Creasey died in Salisbury, UK, in 1973.

Find a full list of our authors and
titles at www.openroadmedia.com

FOLLOW US
@OpenRoadMedia